NO WAY OUT

A steady stream poured in from the top. The mine collapse had allowed water to come in from an underground river or a subterranean pocket. It didn't matter. If there was enough water, it would eventually flood the pocket where Slocum was trapped and he would drown.

Slocum held down his growing panic and backed away. He slipped in the mud forming on the floor. The water level was already midway up his boots. Sloshing around, he thought the collapse might show some other way out of the trap he found himself in. It didn't. The crack had opened up only wide enough to allow the water in.

To fill his little pocket of safety.

"Help! Water's pouring in!" he shouted. His words echoed in the ever-smaller chamber and taunted him. No sounds of rescue came from the other side of the rock fall. Panic overtook him when he realized this was going to be his grave.

Slocum was buried alive . . .

DON'T MISS THESE
ALL-ACTION WESTERN SERIES
FROM THE BERKLEY PUBLISHING GROUP

THE GUNSMITH by J. R. Roberts

Clint Adams was a legend among lawmen, outlaws, and ladies. They called him . . . the Gunsmith.

LONGARM by Tabor Evans

The popular long-running series about Deputy U.S. Marshal Long—his life, his loves, his fight for justice.

SLOCUM by Jake Logan

Today's longest-running action Western. John Slocum rides a deadly trail of hot blood and cold steel.

BUSHWHACKERS by B. J. Lanagan

An action-packed series by the creators of Longarm! The rousing adventures of the most brutal gang of cutthroats ever assembled—Quantrill's Raiders.

DIAMONDBACK by Guy Brewer

Dex Yancey is Diamondback, a Southern gentleman turned con man when his brother cheats him out of the family fortune. Ladies love him. Gamblers hate him. But nobody pulls one over on Dex . . .

WILDGUN by Jack Hanson

The blazing adventures of mountain man Will Barlow—from the creators of Longarm!

TEXAS TRACKER by Tom Calhoun

Meet J.T. Law: the most relentless—and dangerous—manhunter in all Texas. Where sheriffs and posses fail, he's the best man to bring in the most vicious outlaws—for a price.

JAKE LOGAN

SLOCUM
AND THE
HIGH-GRADERS

JOVE BOOKS, NEW YORK

THE BERKLEY PUBLISHING GROUP
Published by the Penguin Group
Penguin Group (USA) Inc.
375 Hudson Street, New York, New York 10014, USA
Penguin Group (Canada), 90 Eglinton Avenue East, Suite 700, Toronto, Ontario M4P 2Y3, Canada
(a division of Pearson Penguin Canada Inc.)
Penguin Books Ltd., 80 Strand, London WC2R 0RL, England
Penguin Group Ireland, 25 St. Stephen's Green, Dublin 2, Ireland (a division of Penguin Books Ltd.)
Penguin Group (Australia), 250 Camberwell Road, Camberwell, Victoria 3124, Australia
(a division of Pearson Australia Group Pty. Ltd.)
Penguin Books India Pvt. Ltd., 11 Community Centre, Panchsheel Park, New Delhi—110 017, India
Penguin Group (NZ), 67 Apollo Drive, Rosedale, North Shore 0745, Auckland, New Zealand
(a division of Pearson New Zealand Ltd.)
Penguin Books (South Africa) (Pty.) Ltd., 24 Sturdee Avenue, Rosebank, Johannesburg 2196,
South Africa

Penguin Books Ltd., Registered Offices: 80 Strand, London WC2R 0RL, England

SLOCUM AND THE HIGH-GRADERS

A Jove Book / published by arrangement with the author

PRINTING HISTORY
Jove edition / July 2007

ISBN: 978-0-515-14321-8

JOVE®
Jove Books are published by The Berkley Publishing Group,
a division of Penguin Group (USA) Inc.,
375 Hudson Street, New York, New York 10014.
JOVE is a registered trademark of Penguin Group (USA) Inc.
The "J" design is a trademark belonging to Penguin Group (USA) Inc.

PRINTED IN THE UNITED STATES OF AMERICA

10 9 8 7 6 5 4 3 2 1

1

John Slocum didn't even have enough money for the fifty-cent whore.

He flattened himself against the long, polished bar as the woman and her paying client pressed close behind, making their way through the crowded saloon to the stairs leading up to the cribs. Slocum reached down and hitched up his gun belt. He had been on the trail so long it felt as if it were a part of him, like an arm—or some other close-at-hand appendage. The ride up from the South had been lonely and unprofitable, and from the look of the miners in the Cripple Creek saloon, he was going to be hard-pressed to change anything of his current impoverished condition.

They were all hard rock men, comfortable working half a mile underground as they scrabbled out a few ounces of gold from the veins running throughout the area. Even as he looked around, the entire building shook and the ground under his feet vibrated. The men never paid a jot of attention, because they knew it wasn't an earthquake. One of the big mines nearby was blasting a new stope.

Slocum ran his fingers over the tall mug of beer. The foam had vanished atop the bitter brew, and it was slowly turning too warm to be palatable. But he wasn't going to rush drinking it; he had spent his last nickel on it.

Looking up, he caught his reflection in the gilt-edged mirror behind the bar and wasn't sure he liked what he saw. He was several shades darker from trail dust, and the heavy lines in his forehead spoke to the long hours in the sun and even longer miles he had ridden throughout the West looking for—

He had no idea what he looked for, other than to see what was over the next hill and beyond the horizon. That was usually good enough, except times like now when his belly growled from lack of food.

Slocum kept looking in the mirror, taking in the bustle behind him. Seven wood tables all had miners crowded around them playing a variety of card games. Along the far wall, a bored-looking woman dealt faro to a pair of miners more interested in seeing if her low-cut dress would slip and give them a better look at her breasts. He suspected she cheated them mercilessly, though they were getting fair value for their money.

Slocum's fingers ran up and down the damp sides of his beer mug as plans formed in his head. He had no money, but he might be able to slip into the right game if there were enough drunken miners willing to lose their hard-earned pay because they had no idea about odds.

His green eyes slowly roved the length of the mirror, from one side to the other, taking in every table, every game, every man in the saloon. It took more than fifteen minutes for him to figure out which table was the most likely to cough up a few dollars.

He touched his vest pocket where his watch rode. He wouldn't risk that in a game. Ever. It was the only legacy he had to remember his brother Robert by. No matter how foolproof—or fool-filled—a poker game might be, he wouldn't put up the watch as his stake. But there were other ways to buy his way in.

With his beer in hand, he swung around, took a sip, then wove his way through the throng trying to get to the far end of the bar, where the whores lined up giving out sweet talk and looks at bare tits for a penny a peek. Now and then a miner with enough money convinced a woman to go up-stairs with him. As drunk as most of the miners were, they wouldn't last long and might even end up robbed and dumped in the alley behind the saloon before anything sexual happened. If it was that kind of place. Slocum hadn't been inside long enough to decide.

"Got room for one more?" Slocum asked, looking over one especially drunk miner's shoulder. The man wove from side to side and would have toppled to the floor if Slocum hadn't put a hand on his shoulder. He almost yanked back when he felt the grime from the greasy shirt caked with dust from deep in the mines rub off onto his hand.

"Got money, you kin join us," spoke up a man across the table. Of the five seated he was the only one who looked sober. His eyes were sharp, hard and bright as the stars in the Colorado sky.

"Don't have money, but I can put up my horse. That mare's worth at least fifty dollars."

"You git the nag onto the table, we'll let you play," said the sober man. Slocum pegged him as a tinhorn gambler, though he was dressed more like a miner. He didn't have the flashy diamond stickpin or other obvious signs that he made his living gambling, but the way his nimble fingers worked to shuffle the deck told Slocum the real story.

"Doubt that'd be possible, though this saloon looks like more 'n one horse has bellied up to the bar."

The man Slocum supported shook as if he had developed a fever. It took Slocum a second to realize he was laughing, not getting ready to die.

"Horse dancin' on the table, goin' up to the bar fer a drink. Thass funny."

"Don't care how talented yer horse is. We're here to play cards."

Slocum had started to debate the point when the drunk jerked free of his grip, turned an unshaven face upward, and peered at him through one eye.

"I need a horse. I'll buy it."

"Jed, don't—" the gambler started, then settled down to a slow shuffle when he saw the drunk was going to buy Slocum's horse no matter what. Once a man's brain is pickled enough, getting an idea to leave is damn near impossible.

"Fifty dollars is a good price," Slocum said. "If I get lucky, I'll buy the horse back for twice that. You'd double your money in a couple hours."

"Do tell," the drunk said. He fished around in his vest pocket and found a tiny twenty-dollar gold piece. That seemed to be all the money he had on him.

"That's a bargain you're getting," Slocum said, taking the coin. "I'll buy the horse back for fifty. That's more than twice your money."

"More 'n twice? Cain't get odds like that nowhere else." Those were the man's last coherent words. He slumped away from Slocum and hit the floor hard enough to rival the earlier boom from the mine blast. Nobody in the saloon took note. Slocum stepped over him and sat down, spinning the coin, which was hardly the size of the fingernail on his little finger, so that it shone brilliantly.

"What's yer pleasure, mister?" the gambler asked.

"Five card draw's good as anything."

"Not Red Dog?"

"Five card draw," Slocum insisted. "That makes us all equal in the betting." He didn't want the gambler to act as dealer and bank. Slocum wanted to be able to get money from the others at the table.

That's what he wanted. And for the first few hands that's what he got. Slowly, surely, he added to the pile of silver coins and crumpled greenbacks on the table in front of him until he was feeling downright comfortable again. A quick count showed him to be more than a hundred dollars ahead.

"Here," Slocum said, taking fifty in almost worthless paper money from the table. He started to stuff it into the unconscious man's pocket so he could claim his horse again. That'd mean he was still up seventy dollars, most of it in gold and silver.

"You don't want to do that," the gambler said. "Otherwise, you're gonna lose the pot. I'm puttin' it all in. You either call, raise—or fold."

The man was as good as his word. He pushed tall stacks of chips and specie into the pot and then sat back, looking smug. Slocum needed the fifty dollars to call. He laid his hands flat over his cards. There was no reason to study them again. The dirty cards were burned into his mind. How often did he get a full house, queens over tens? He had watched the gambler like a hawk and knew the man was aware of his scrutiny. If the gambler had dealt himself anything to beat this hand, he was a better cheat than Slocum gave him credit for.

"I'll call."

"Reckon I got to fold," the gambler said, surprising Slocum.

"That was easier than I thought," Slocum said, reaching for the pot.

"Hold on, mister. There's still one more in the game."

The gambler looked to the man to his right, who suddenly didn't appear as drunk as he had even a few seconds earlier. Slocum felt as if he had just fallen down a well. He had watched the gambler for dealing seconds or off the bottom—to himself. Slocum had not considered the idea that the gambler worked with a partner.

"I'm callin'," the formerly drunk miner said. "And I'm winnin'. Ain't no hand that kin beat mine." He laid down a royal flush. "Them's the purtiest hearts I ever did see."

Slocum tossed his hand into the center of the table.

"Got me beat," he admitted. The gambler and his cohort both smiled. The other miners at the table were so far into their cups they didn't know what was going on. The one who had bought Slocum's horse stirred and sat up.

"Whass goin' on?"

"Jed, you want to sell that horse you bought? I'll give you five dollars and a bottle of tarantula juice for it," the gambler said.

"A whole damn bottle?"

The gambler called to the barkeep for a full bottle and

took the money from the pile in front of his partner. Then he separated out five greasy single dollar bills and tossed them to Jed, who grabbed for them, catching one and sending the other four fluttering into the room, where they vanished like dew in the morning sun.

"Your bottle," the gambler said, taking it from the bartender and handing it to Jed. The miner greedily sucked up the potent whiskey.

To Slocum the gambler said, "'Less you got more money, why don't you free up that there chair fer somebody else? And which horse is yers?" The gambler laughed and amended, "Which of them nags *was* yers?"

Slocum considered describing the wrong horse, but that would be the same as stealing another man's horse.

"I need to get my tack," he said. "The horse'll be the one without a saddle or saddlebags."

The gambler inclined his head. His partner got to his feet, rested his hand on the butt of a six-shooter, and indicated that Slocum was to precede him from the saloon.

Without a word, Slocum left. He had been suckered like a greenhorn, and it was his own fault. He should have bought back his horse and gotten out of the game when he was ahead. Now he was not only broke but on foot.

He stepped into the cold night mountain air. Tethered at the end of the boardwalk, his horse whinnied.

"That the one?" asked the man behind him.

"She's the one." Slocum unfastened his saddle and slung it over his shoulder, staggering a little under the weight. Other than the beer, he hadn't put anything into his belly since sunup, more hours back than he could remember now.

"Much obliged," the gambler's crony said, shooing the horse down the street and running to keep up. Slocum figured the horse would be sold for a few dollars, in spite of being a decent mount, and the man would return so he and the gambler could fleece someone else. Slocum touched the butt of his six-gun but knew there was no point in making a fuss. He had been stupid and it had cost him. Maybe memory of this night would keep him from making the same mistake again.

He walked slowly down Cripple Creek's main street. The first light of dawn turned the ridge of mountains to the east a pearly color, but Slocum's eyes weren't on the sunrise but on the freighters rattling down the street. Three of them. Two rode in the back with shotguns resting in the crooks of their arms.

Drawn like a fly to shit, he followed to the edge of town, where half a dozen more men, all armed with six-shooters and rifles, stood guard over a small pile covered with a tarp. Slocum smelled gold waiting to be shipped. He dropped his saddle on the boardwalk and fussed with it, all the while watching how the men handled themselves—and the gold.

The longer he watched, the more his spirits sank. They worked like a well-trained squad of soldiers. Three of the riflemen walked to the front of the wagon and the other three to the rear. The shotgun guards jumped down and stood on either side of the hidden gold until the driver got down, grumbling about aching joints, and pulled back the tarp.

Slocum's heart jumped in his chest. There was enough gold there to make him a rich man. There were also nine men who looked as likely to shoot him as to ask what he wanted if he got within fifty feet. He continued to watch as the driver counted the gold bars, then barked out an order to his two guards.

Only then did the shotguns get laid down. The men joked as they loaded the gold into the middle of the wagon bed, but for all their joviality, Slocum saw that neither of the men had turned careless. They loaded the gold—they also kept a watch out for anyone too close. It didn't matter that the six riflemen were on duty. The three with the wagon remained alert.

Too alert.

Slocum sat on the boardwalk, watching and thinking. There wasn't any way a lone robber could get at the gold here. Out on the road to Denver? Maybe. Three men gave better odds than nine, but how was he to ride out and set an ambush when he didn't even have a horse?

Papers were swapped and the driver climbed into the box, complaining loudly about his arthritis and how cold it was this early in the day. For all his complaints, he was as watchful as any of the others. He checked to be certain both his cargo and the two guards were in place before getting the rig moving. Wood groaned and leather creaked as the horses began pulling the wagon along the road that wound its way through the Rockies and ended up at some bank in Denver. A bank with a secure vault.

The gold-laden wagon vanished from sight, and Slocum still sat on the boardwalk trying to figure a way that some of the precious metal could end up in his pocket. He sat for another hour and watched another wagon pull out with a cargo of gold before becoming disconsolate. There was no way he could ever hold up one of those shipments. The first had three guards, but the gold was carried in an open wagon. The second shipment went out in what amounted to an armored stagecoach. That was bad, but the two guards inside with their rifles poking out through narrow windows was worse. It would take an entire army company to rob that shipment.

Slocum's attention drifted from the gold shipments to the ebb and flow of miners. Just before the sun peeked above the mountains, steam whistles had blown, summoning the workers to their mines. He considered the businesses left virtually deserted in town now as likely sources of money. Robbing men who needed the money as much as he did—and who worked hard for it—rankled. If the mines lost an entire shipment, it would be an irritation but not a tragedy for the owners.

But there seemed to be hardly any place that fit his twisted morality that wasn't heavily guarded. Cripple

Creek was a typical boomtown with crime running rampant. Few of the businesses seemed to have much faith in the local marshal, and most employed their own guards. This got Slocum to thinking about taking a job as guard somewhere.

He walked the streets hunting for a likely enterprise that would need a tough hombre to keep the drunks out and the money in the till, and ended up in front of the Lucky Dollar Saloon.

He went inside and looked around. It was like any other saloon he had ever seen, except the painting of the naked woman behind the bar was artistically a little better and the bar was polished to a mirror sheen.

"What kin I git for you, mister?" The barkeep popped up from behind the bar and laid a six-gun down.

"I'm looking for a job. You need a bouncer to keep order?"

"Nope." The bartender's hand inched toward his weapon.

"Not at this instant, but when the miners come pouring in all thirsty and wanting to get liquored up, that can be a different can of worms," Slocum said. He saw another man standing in a doorway leading to a back room. He couldn't be certain, but he thought the man held a sawed-off shotgun down at his side.

"Don't need help," the barkeep said.

"I'm a hard worker," Slocum said. "If you're not in the hiring mood right now, do you know somewhere that is?"

"Nope. You git on outta here, 'less you want to order."

"If I had that much money, I wouldn't need a job."

Slocum hefted his gear and left, going from store to store for more than two hours and getting the same reception everywhere he stopped. He had never seen a town less friendly or inclined to put a man to work, even mucking the stables. The inquiry at the livery had been prompted by the wild-ass notion he might work there and find a horse to steal. Horse-stealing was as lowdown as a man could get, but Slocum was scraping the bottom of the barrel. But even the stable owner had turned down his offer to work.

Slocum had been down and out before, but there had usually been a bright spot on the horizon. Not now. He considered tracking down the gamblers who had cheated him and forcing some settlement, but the time for that was long past by now. And, truth to tell, he had a sneaking admiration for the way they had suckered him into betting all his money against a stacked deck.

He trooped along, hunting for some store where he hadn't already inquired after a job, when the ground shook. This explosion was so intense it forced him to his knees. Almost immediately a whistle blew and the sound of frightened men reached his ears.

Slocum swung his saddle over his shoulder and followed the commotion to the north end of town. Many of the mines had entrances there, going straight into the sides of mountains, where the miners followed the elusive veins of gold ever deeper into solid rock. Slocum had no trouble finding which mine had succumbed to disaster. Huge plumes of dust billowed from the elevator shaft of the Low Down Mine.

The whistle kept up a steady screech that deafened Slocum. Then the ground opened up under his feet and he plunged downward into dust-filled darkness.

2

Slocum fell for what seemed an eternity, then hit the ground so hard it knocked the wind from his lungs. Gasping, sucking in dirt, he struggled to sit up. It took him several seconds to realize he was facedown in the dirt. Through force of will, he rolled over, covering his face against a rain of stones pelting him from above. Then there was nothing but utter silence. No more rocks. No falling grit. Nothing.

He sat up and wiped at his face using his bandanna until he was breathing more normally. His chest hurt as badly as if he had been shot, and his legs throbbed from the impact of his fall. Tying the bandanna over his mouth and face let him suck in deep breaths without the dust clogging his nose and throat. Standing was a chore, but he got to his feet, bracing himself against an unseen wall.

The silence began to fade as harsh cries of dying men reached his ears. Slocum looked up and saw the blue Colorado dawn fifteen feet above. As his eyes adjusted to the darkness, he saw he had fallen into a tunnel. An underground blast had caused the cave-in, and he had been unlucky enough to be standing directly over the collapsing mine shaft. Stumbling forward, he got over the fist-sized rocks littering the stope and worked his way upward to a small chamber lit by a dozen carbide lamps and more miner's candles than he could count. The men gathered around looked grim. One saw Slocum and demanded, "What the hell are you doing here? You're not a miner."

"The ground up and swallowed me," Slocum said. "What happened? Somebody put down too big a charge?"

"We got problems right now, mister. Get on over to the elevator and they'll take you out."

"Suits me, but I lost my gear in the fall."

"I'll see to it later, after we get a couple men out from behind a big plug of rock."

The man turned and pointedly ignored Slocum. Slocum saw that the big, burly miner was poring over a map of the underground empire devoted only to retrieving gold and knew he was as useless as teats on a bull. He considered returning to the spot where he had fallen into the mine and hunting for his saddle and other gear, then pushed it from his mind. Better to get aboveground and wait. If an errant blast had caused a cave-in, there was no telling where the mine tunnels had been weakened.

Tromping through the dust and large, sharp pieces of rock that had dislodged from both the walls and roof, Slocum reached the elevator cage. The operator blinked when he saw him.

"The foreman told me to get aboveground," Slocum said.

"I don't know where you came from, but you're headed in the right direction." The operator jerked his thumb upward. "Climb on in and let's get out of this hellhole."

The miner rang a bell, got a reply from the operator above, then held on as the cage, which was hardly more than a platform, began shivering, shaking, and lurching to the surface. As they came to a halt, Slocum spilled out, glad to be out of the mine shaft.

"Thanks," he told the operator.

"If I was you, I'd stay here. It's closer to Heaven than anywhere down there." The operator jerked his thumb downward, grinned, white teeth shining from the middle of a filthy face, then vanished as the cage lowered once more.

"What happened?" a young man asked Slocum.

"I don't rightly know, but from the sound of it and from my fall, I'd say there was a premature detonation. Too much explosive went off at the wrong time and some of the mine shafts began collapsing."

The young man scribbled furiously, then said, "Thanks. This is going to be the lead in today's paper. My first headline!"

Without waiting for Slocum to say anything more, he ran away in the direction of Cripple Creek's distant main street. Slocum sagged down. He had wanted to tell the young reporter that he wasn't even a miner and that his only interest in the Low Down Mine was in retrieving his gear.

He walked slowly to the spot where the ground had caved in. Slocum cautiously peered down but couldn't see his saddle or other gear. He backed away, careful not to cause the lip of the hole to collapse further.

The whistle had stopped and the furious crush of men hurrying to the mine to help their trapped friends faded away until it wasn't possible to tell that anything untoward had happened. Slocum settled down on an empty keg of Giant Blasting Powder and waited. A couple hours later, the elevator cage rattled back to the surface. Four miners dragged tarps from the platform. Slocum knew from the ominous shapes that they carried what remained of the trapped miners.

Coming over to him was the miner Slocum had pegged as the foreman.

The man looked grim enough to carry the burdens of the world on his shoulders. Slocum suspected the miner was mostly concerned about the deaths.

"I sent a mucker to find your gear. Sorry that you got dropped down like that."

"I came out better than they did. That all of them?" Slocum looked to the tarp shrouds.

"What we could find of them."

"Too much powder? Or was it a spark that set off the blast prematurely?"

"You sound like you know something about blasting."

Slocum shrugged.

"You want a job? I need four assistant blasters right now."

"You have a master? Or is that you?"

"I'm Thompson and I'm in charge of the blasting. But that wasn't my fault. The four assistants were sent to blast by the foreman."

"And he didn't bother telling you?"

Thompson spat. His dark eyes fixed on Slocum. "I don't dodge my own mistakes. If I made one, it was not trainin' them boys better so they could work without supervision."

"That'd make them masters, wouldn't it?"

Thompson laughed without humor. He wiped more grit from his face, spat, and then said, "Pay's rotten. Hours are long. Work's damned dangerous, as you can see. There's something about workin' in a mine that's like workin' in your very own grave."

"You make it sound mighty unattractive," Slocum said.

"Them's the good points," Thompson said. "You can guess what the bad ones are." He glanced toward the bodies.

"How much?"

"Dollar a day and all the rock you can eat. Bonuses for new veins, bonuses for ever' day minimum production is exceeded, bonuses for bein' on the job at the end of a month and a year."

"Who's gotten the year-end bonus?" Slocum asked.

"Ain't many," Thompson admitted, "but I'm one. Mr. Haining is a decent mine owner, compared with most others in Cripple Creek."

"Haining? Does he get down into the mine himself, or does he sit behind a big cherrywood desk over in Denver?"

Thompson looked at Slocum funny. He spat, then said, "He don't get down into the mine himself, but he's not just an owner. He takes a personal interest. That's his office over there on that rise, if you want to go talk to him."

"Reckon he's a mite busy at the moment," Slocum said.

"He writes letters to any family a miner has. Don't know he'll write more 'n one from this crew, though."

"No family?"

"How about you?"

Slocum laughed and said, "Mr. Haining won't have to write a letter on my account. I don't figure on dying."

"Who does? But you're hired. Now, what's your name?"

Slocum introduced himself and asked about room and board.

"Ain't high on the list of most owners, but Mr. Haining lets out a boardinghouse."

Slocum tensed. He had heard of dealings like this before. The owner paid a substandard wage, then forced his employees to buy from a company store or stay in rundown housing and ended up with the small money paid out in salary.

"A dime a day," Thompson said. "Not much, not very good, but affordable. And better than letting it rain and snow on your head all night long."

"That's it?"

"Breakfast is included. No dinner, and any food you take down into the mine is paid for out of your pocket."

"I'm liking this better and better. How is it that I can't get a job anywhere in Cripple Creek, and something this good goes wanting?"

"Dangerous," Thompson said. He eyed Slocum's cross-draw holster and the worn ebony butt of the Colt Navy resting there. "Then again, bein' dangerous ain't much of a problem for you, is it?"

"Not now that I have my gear back." Slocum saw a scrawny, towheaded boy struggling to drag the saddle with the saddlebags still tied on. He went and hoisted the saddle to his shoulder, nodded thanks to the boy, and went back to where Thompson waited. "Where do I go?"

"Up the hill until you see the Low Down sign. That's the

bunkhouse. Then you get your cracker ass back down here. There's still four hours left in the shift, and I've got blasting to do."

Slocum got his gear stowed, reluctantly tucked his Colt Navy and gun belt in the middle of his bedroll, then hurried back to the mouth of the mine, where Thompson waited impatiently.

"You have experience with explosives, or were you just blowin' off words to impress me?"

"I've handled powder and nitro," Slocum said simply. The answer, stripped of any bragging, impressed Thompson.

"Let's get on down and go to work. There're miner's lamps below."

They rattled and clanked all the way down to the level where Slocum had fallen. He took a deep breath when the elevator kept going lower, much lower. Counting levels, Slocum was about ready to give up when the platform stopped at twenty-three. He guessed they were more than three hundred feet below the surface.

"Here," Thompson said, tossing Slocum a helmet with a carbide lamp on it. The man waited as Slocum quickly checked it, added water from an open cask nearby, and got the carbide lamp burning. "You got the look of an experienced miner. Let's see if you've got what it takes to be a powder monkey."

Slocum had to walk slightly bent over since the roof was only an inch above his six-foot height, but he was more concerned with the way the drift turned this way and that like a snake. The rock was cold and wet to the touch. He shivered and wished he had worn his coat. Next shift. He only had four hours to go on this one.

"That there's Billy, and the other fellow, the one without an eye, that's Bowden. Don't know if he's got a first name, since I never asked and he never supplied one."

Slocum took in the other men. Billy hadn't been shaving too long but looked years older than his real age. He was short, stocky, and solemn. Bowden was everything Billy wasn't. Even taller than Slocum and thinner than a slat, he never seemed to rest. If he wasn't shuffling his feet, his hands were darting this way and that, rubbing up and down his canvas pants or across the sleeves of his flannel shirt. The eye not hidden by a tattered, filthy patch moved restlessly, sometimes going in a direction opposite to the way he turned his head. Not much hair remained on the top of Bowden's head, but it was hardly needed. Slocum had never seen so many scars on a man before as the number crisscrossing Bowden's head.

"We got to blow free the rubble from the last blast?" Bowden pointed down the drift, his long, bony fingers fluttering as if some unseen breeze ruffled them.

"That's what Mr. Miles wants," Thompson said.

"That the foreman?"

"You are a greenhorn if you don't know that," Billy said. "Yep, Lucas Miles, God's gift to the underground. He's one—"

"Shut up, Billy," Thompson said. "Don't go bad-mouthin' our boss."

"Mr. Haining's our boss, not Miles," grumbled the youth.

"Miles hires and fires. He could fire your ass in a flash if he chose to."

"Might as well fire me as bury me. It's his doin' that cost four lives today, and you know it, Thompson."

"I told you to shut up."

"So fire me. Or get Miles to do it." Billy looked truculent. He thrust out his chin as if daring the blaster to hit him. "You need me. Hell, you need us all. We do the work of three men. And if you're hirin' men like him, that means nobody else'll work for Miles."

"I can pull my own weight," Slocum said.

"Sorry," Billy said. "Didn't mean that you were a slacker. No slackers down here, 'cept for Miles."

"Enough. You show Slocum where the tools're kept, then get to the end of the new drift and start drilling. Me and Bowden will fix up a charge."

"Come on," Billy said, gesturing to Slocum. They walked in silence down the drift to a larger chamber where bits and sledgehammers were scattered around. Billy checked several of the six-foot-long steel bits until he found one with a properly sharpened tip. "Damn things are never sharpened," he said. "Miles lets his cronies get by with murder. We work hard and all they do is lollygag and get drunk."

"You don't cotton much to the foreman, do you?"

"No reason to. He treats everyone like dirt, then sucks up to Mr. Haining. He hires his friends and hardly ever pokes his ugly face down into the mine."

"You blame Thompson for that?"

"Thompson? Hell no, he's a good guy. Hard worker and the best powderman you'll find in any mine, bar none. If Mr. Haining didn't need him so much to do the blasting, he'd be foreman. But Mr. Haining's more concerned with money matters than anything goin' on here."

"Seems wrong," Slocum said. He picked up a twelve-pound sledgehammer and followed Billy down a drift. Their lights bobbed about, showing increasingly ragged walls. This section was newly blasted and hadn't been exploited yet. Shiny flecks shone in his light as Slocum looked around. Gold. Lots of it.

"The Low Down's a good mine," Billy said. "If things were like they ought to be, Miles would be in jail."

"In jail? For being a lousy foreman?"

Billy snorted. He positioned a couple miner's candles on either side of a rock plug blocking the end of the drift and rubbed his callused finger over a spot marked with a chalk X.

"There's a difference 'tween bein' a wastrel and bein' a criminal. I got to worry when so many accidents happen, all intended to cripple the Low Down."

"You're saying that Miles is responsible?"

"I'm sayin' not many of the deaths look much like an accident. Men get careless, it happens," he assured Slocum. "But those four killed today? Mighty suspicious circumstances, I'd say. And I put it directly on Miles's doorstep."

Billy picked up the long steel rod and positioned the chisel point where the X had been scrawled. He looked back at Slocum.

"You want to hold the bit, or you want to swing the hammer?"

Slocum knew which was harder and which was more dangerous.

"You're the old hand at this."

Billy nodded. "You're no greenhorn, either. You know how bunged up you can get holding the bit. Me, I'm not as strong, and that'd make my hammering a little wobbly after a spell. I'll hold, you swing."

Slocum stepped back, took the heavy sledgehammer, and waited for Billy to position it where the hole was to be drilled. When they had a four- or five-foot-deep hole, they'd move to another portion of the wall and put in another and then another and another.

Then the explosive would be packed into the new holes and a new segment of mountain would be turned into gravel. At that point, muckers would load the debris and get it out of the mine to be sorted and sent to the mill for crushing and the smelter for refining into gold bricks. A good strike meant a few ounces of gold for every ton of rock moved from the belly of the Earth.

After only four hours, Slocum was ready to go off shift. The work was backbreaking, but he liked Billy and Bowden and got along just fine with Thompson. He thought he was going to enjoy working in the Low Down Mine.

3

The work was backbreaking, but Slocum found he enjoyed it because he was able to get a few dollars ahead while working with men he respected. Billy might have been a considerable number of years younger than Slocum, but he knew his trade. Bowden was as crazy as a loon and made the most of it, peering at people with his wandering good eye until they flinched. It took a while to warm to him, but when they got to swapping lies, Bowden proved to be both expert and astute. Thompson was a bit more aloof, but he made certain the men working under him were well taken care of. Or as well taken care of as any miner in the Cripple Creek district.

The work was done in cold, dark tunnels barely wide enough for Slocum to pass along without brushing his shoulders. He had to constantly bend over, and more than once he found himself on the edge of an unmarked pit. If he had stepped into the darkness, he would have landed on the next level down in a pile of broken bones—his bones.

But he got into the rhythm of swinging the heavy sledgehammer and eventually worked over to holding the chisel as others hammered away. Of the two, Slocum preferred using the sledge rather than wondering if the one wielding the heavy hammer would miss and crush his hands. In spite of the dangers, they had blasted and torn out close to thirty feet of new drift by the end of the second week Slocum had been working.

"Got to tell you, men," Thompson said to them as they ate their lunch, "you've been burning up the mountain. Nobody else is making this much progress."

"Yeah, but there ain't no gold in the rock. We're followin' a damn will-o'-the-wisp," Bowden declared. He held out his roast beef sandwich so the light from his carbide lamp fell on it. Slocum looked away. The meat was tinged with green even in good light; it turned putrid in the curiously bright carbide glare, but this didn't stop Bowden from munching away at it.

"The big vein we hit last month turned in that direction," Thompson said.

They all looked up when Lucas Miles and two of his cronies came trooping into their rocky chamber.

"Yeah, we been wonderin' 'bout that," Miles said. "Not bringin' out the gold you were."

"Hell, Miles, not every rock has gold in it. You know that."

"I been thinkin' might be a lot of gold in that rock, but none of it's gettin' to the surface."

"Nobody here's stealin' the gold," Thompson said hotly.

"I ain't accusin' nobody. I just want to make sure some dust ain't fallin' into pockets unbeknownst to them," Miles growled. His two men turned to Bowden. "Let 'em search you," Miles ordered.

"Like hell I will."

"Do it or I'll fire you," Miles said. He glared at Thompson to shut him up.

"You want to see what's in my pockets?" Billy spoke up.

"We'll get to you, boy."

"Here, look now. It's the only chance you're gonna get." Billy turned his pockets inside out and spun slowly. "You want to look at my boots? They got holes in the soles, so I'd be leavin' a gold trail behind."

"He's clean, boss," one man said after checking Billy's clothing.

"Go on, Bowden, show us you ain't got nuthin' to hide," Miles said.

Slocum watched carefully. These men weren't going to search him. Either they took his word or they fired him. He had come to enjoy the work, at least as much as a mole might, but he wouldn't put up with such accusations. Then he had to keep from laughing when he saw Bowden dancing around in the harsh light from the miner's lamps.

Bowden stripped off his shirt and tossed it to the floor. His boots followed. Then he skinned out of his pants so he was dressed only in his longjohns. But the half-crazy man didn't stop there. He pulled off the woollies and dropped them onto the pile. He stood buck naked and shivering until his pallid white skinned turned blue from the cold.

"You got a razor on you, Miles?" Bowden asked.

Miles looked stunned at the man stripping down to his bare skin. He shook his head and said, "No. Why are you askin' a thing like that?"

"I reckon you want to shave the fur off my hairy hide and see if I've woven gold into my beard. And back here. You want to check here, too, Miles?" Bowden swung around and bent over, presenting his hindquarters to the foreman. "You might see somethin' you like there. If it's gold, let me know. If it's somethin' else, don't bother tellin' me." He waggled his rear like a cancan dancer.

"Let's get out of here," Miles said.

"Hold on," Thompson called to the foreman. "You're forgettin' something, Miles."

"What?"

"An apology."

"Go to hell," Miles snarled. He stormed off, his two henchmen trailing behind him. One cast a final look at Bowden, who danced about in his birthday suit, then shook his head and went around a bend in the drift.

"Get dressed, you stupid son of a bitch," Thompson said.

"I dunno, boss, I kinda like it this way. Makes me feel all free." Bowden spun about with his hands above his head.

"It makes me sick to my belly." Thompson turned away but Slocum saw the smile on his lips. He appreciated the way Bowden had humiliated Miles after the foreman's accusation that they were smuggling gold from the Low Down.

While Bowden climbed back into his clothes, Slocum and Billy finished their lunches. Slocum chased his with a swig of water from his canteen.

"Time to get back to work, gents," Thompson said. "And don't you go stealin' gold from the mine, now."

"We got to find it first," Billy said. "I think we're gettin' closer, though, to that big vein."

"Me and Bowden'll hit it first. The new drift looks promisin', and we're about ready to blast."

"Need help?" Billy asked.

"That'll be the day, when I need your help. You just want an excuse to stand around and watch instead of workin'. Get to it, you two."

With that, Thompson and Bowden set off down an adjoining drift. Billy hoisted a long, steel chisel and pointed to the sledgehammer.

"You want to hammer a spell? My shoulder's botherin' me something fierce again."

Slocum silently picked up the twelve-pound hammer, and they went back down the drift where they had worked so hard for the past ten days. He was no geologist, but the rock here looked promising for more gold. Slocum hadn't seen the drift where Thompson and Bowden were commencing to blast.

"Wait up," Slocum said. "I left my canteen back there. I get mighty thirsty pounding on the end of that spike."

"You should work out in the hot sun drivin' railroad spikes," Billy said. "I did that for almost three months on the Denver & Rio Grande. No way would I give up this job to get out into fresh air. We lost more crews to avalanches than you can shake a stick at."

Slocum dropped his hammer, then backtracked, his stride long and gliding as he kept hunched over. He reached the chamber and grabbed his canteen, then paused. From the drift where Thompson and Bowden had gone he heard a commotion. Before he could figure out what the men were doing, it stopped. Slocum shrugged off the echoes; his ears still played tricks on him, even after being underground for so long. Vibrations moved through rock and down drifts and up stopes in ways his tracking skills told him were impossible. Despite what Billy said, Slocum wouldn't mind seeing the open ranges and tall mountains again, rather than the confined spaces of a gold mine.

Slocum hurried back to where Billy stood studying the wall.

"Thompson's marked where he thinks we ought to drill," Billy said. "You reckon these are good places?"

"He knows what he's doing," Slocum said. He examined the four spots where Thompson had drawn chalk marks, then shrugged. "As good as anyplace, though if we moved this hole over about eight inches it might blast through the rock better." Slocum traced out the strata showing harder segments.

"You've got the touch, too, Slocum," Billy said. "Let's start there. I don't think Thompson would mind. He's—"

The explosion that rumbled through the mine knocked both men to the ground. Slocum's carbide lamp went flying, spilling the water and the calcium carbide pellets to the ground. They sizzled and hissed, but Slocum couldn't hear them. The explosion had deafened him. He fumbled around, lost his balance, and sat heavily. His head spun, and getting his feet under him proved impossible.

He had felt this way before. Sudden shocks caused his balance to gallop away whenever he went deaf. Slocum propped himself up against the wall and let the dizziness pass. He looked around the gloom and saw Billy fumbling to get a miner's candle lit. Several strikes of a lucifer finally ignited the wick and cast a yellow light around.

"What happened?" the young miner said.

Slocum saw Billy's lips moving but knew he heard less than he guessed.

"Explosion," Slocum shouted. "We don't have any powder, so it must have been either Thompson or the magazine."

"We'd be goners if the magazine had blowed," Billy said.

A buzzing sound began to invade Slocum's skull, and slowly his normal hearing returned. He got to his feet and stumbled along behind the miner as they made their way to the chamber where they had split with Thompson and Bowden. Every step took Slocum through thicker clouds of dust until he was choking. He pulled off his bandanna and slung it over his nose and mouth, as if he were enduring a West Texas sandstorm. His eyes watered, but he kept Billy's flickering candle in sight. Even so, he crashed into the young man when he stopped suddenly.

"We gotta get out of here," Billy said. "The entire drift where Thompson was blasting is gone. The whole level might collapse."

"We can't leave him and Bowden," Slocum said. He took the candle and went to the mouth of the tunnel. Holding the light high let him see how the roof had collapsed. "There's room enough for me to get through."

"There might be damp, Slocum. You could blow yerself up like they did."

Slocum knew "damp" was a constant concern. The explosive gas might be released at any time from reservoirs trapped in the rock. It was deadly to breathe and worse if an explosion opened a pocket.

"Then you hold the candle," Slocum said, handing it back to Billy.

"Hell, man, you can't go into that without light. You wouldn't know if there was a pit opened up in front of you."

"Then give me your miner's lamp."

"That can be as bad as open flame. Oh, hell, you're bound and determined, ain't you, Slocum?" Billy handed over his carbide lamp. Slocum settled the sweat-stained leather band around his forehead, then began scrambling to get past the rockfall.

He found a level area just beyond. And no gaping cavity intent on swallowing him alive. He made good speed through the clogged, dusty drift and then stopped dead in his tracks when he saw boots ahead sticking out from under a segment of fallen roof.

"Bowden," Slocum called. He tugged on the boots, and the legs came free. Sharp stone had severed them at the knees. Slocum swallowed hard and shined his light around, fearing what he would find next.

A bloody, broken hand thrust out from under the same rock that had killed Bowden. Slocum recognized the hand as Thompson's. He began scraping away debris, but there was no point. The powderman had been crushed like a bug.

Slocum was loath to pull on the hand because he feared the result would be the same as tugging on Bowden's boots. But he saw something bright and shiny clenched in the hand. He pried it open and saw a silver Mexican concha.

He held it up and looked at it, wondering where it had come from. Thompson didn't strike him as the sort to go in for such finery, even if could have afforded it.

"Slocum, you all right?"

"I found them," he called. "Both Thompson and Bowden are dead."

"Then get out of there. The elevator's gonna take us up. Miles is worried about the whole level collapsin'."

"Fancy that," Slocum said. "The foreman actually worried about losing a couple more miners."

"Who knows? He might have to pay for the tombstones. Now get out of there."

Slocum tucked the concha into his pocket and wormed his way through the tight fit that got him back to where Billy stood. Three other miners looked on, their expressions telling what they felt and thought of Thompson and Bowden getting killed. They weren't men inclined to tears, but Slocum saw how close they came to bawling.

"Next stop, fresh air," Billy said, taking Slocum's arm and hurrying him along. "You sure both Thompson and Bowden are goners?"

"Caught under a rock that fell from the roof," Slocum said. "They never had a chance."

"Damn, but it hurts to lose them. Especially Thompson. He was a good man." Billy then clamped his mouth shut, looked at the rock moving slowly past as they were carried to the surface, and didn't say another word.

They reached the surface and stepped out into a drizzling rain. Slocum couldn't have picked more appropriate weather. It matched his gray mood.

"Hey, you, Slocum, isn't it? Come on over here," bellowed Lucas Miles. The foreman stood under a canvas canopy with his two assistants.

"You going to dig them out?" Slocum asked.

"What? Oh, you mean the dead miners? Do you think it's worth our time?"

"They deserve more than being left down there for the worms," Slocum said. "Besides, Thompson thought that drift was most likely where the vein of gold had meandered to from the main diggings."

"Then we open it back up. Herk and Singer will see to it, but they don't know blasting. You do, don't you, Slocum?"

Slocum only nodded. He was eyeing Herk closer. The man had his hat pushed back so his forehead shone in the light from a lamp on a table nearby, but an occasional glint caught Slocum's eye like a raven spying a gewgaw.

"Whatcha starin' at?" the hulking man said. Herk pulled his hat back down, exposing the hatband.

"You get that hat in Mexico?" Slocum asked.

"Took it off a dead Mexican," Herk said.

"I like the silver work on the band, though you're missing a concha."

"The hell you say!" Herk yanked off his hat and turned it around. "I never noticed. Musta lost it recently. I had it this morning."

"Maybe you lost it in the mine," Slocum said. He fingered the matching silver concha in his pocket.

"Yeah, might—"

"Herk's not been down in the mine," Miles said.

"Sure he was," Slocum said in a level tone. "When you accused Bowden of stealing nuggets."

"Yeah, right, but that don't matter now. Look, Slocum, Thompson said some good things about you and said you knew your way around explosives. That so?" Miles fixed a cold stare on him that Slocum returned.

"Reckon that's true."

"Then I'm promotin' you to master blaster. You're head powderman down there, and your first chore is figurin' how to get the bodies out, then continuin' with the blasting down that drift."

Slocum kept fingering the concha in his pocket, then dropped his hand to his side.

"What's it pay?"

"Twice what you're gettin' now," Miles said.

"I'm your man," Slocum said. He thrust out his hand for Miles to shake. The foreman hesitated, then glared at Slocum and finally shook.

"Deal," Miles said. "See that you're a sight more careful with the powder than your predecessor."

"I'm a real careful man," Slocum said. He smiled and none of the three men returned it.

4

"Hey, Slocum, the boss wants you."

Slocum glanced up at Herk from the sheets showing the inventory of blasting powder. The burly man stood with his arms crossed over his barrel chest and looking as if the summons forced him to exert himself too much. He hadn't done a damned thing around the mine otherwise.

"I need to finish this list. Tell Miles I'll be along shortly."

"Ain't Miles what wants you. It's Mr. Haining. You'd better get your ass up the hill right now. He don't like to be kept waitin'."

Slocum glanced at the tallies, then tucked the sheet into his shirt pocket. He could finish it later. Talking with the mine owner wasn't something he wanted to do, but he knew it had to be done eventually.

He followed the direction Herk pointed, then began trooping up the steep hill toward a shack emblazoned with a neatly painted sign telling one and all that this was the Low Down Mine HQ. Slocum hesitated at the door, then knocked. He had no idea how much of a stickler Morgan Haining was, but getting off on the wrong foot with him wouldn't accomplish much.

"Come on in. The door's unlatched," came a pleasant

voice from inside. Slocum pushed his way in and saw a well-dressed man sitting behind a desk, papers spread in a wide fan in front of him. Two inkwells were strategically placed on the right side of the desk, with a bevy of quill pens around them.

"You must be the new master powderman."

"Slocum, sir."

"Don't just stand there, come on in and have a seat. The office isn't much, but I don't see any reason to put a lot of money into something like this, do you?"

"Money's better spent in the mine," Slocum said.

"Exactly, exactly, Mr. Slocum. You're my kind of man. But I knew you were, since you came so highly recommended. Drink?" Haining opened the bottom desk drawer and pulled out a bottle of Billy Taylor's finest whiskey, the seal still intact on the cork. Slocum doubted this was one of the fake bottles he saw at the town saloons and was, instead, the real thing.

"It's been a while since I had a decent shot of whiskey. I'd like that," Slocum said.

"Then here you go," Haining said, pouring into a single shot glass. Slocum wondered whether the Low Down's owner was going to drink straight from the bottle. Instead, he stuck the cork back in. Seeing Slocum's attention, he explained, "I can't drink like I used to. Ulcer. As much as I fancy a drink now and then, it tears up my gut. But don't let that stop you. You look as if you need to cut the dust with a good drink."

Slocum knocked back the whiskey and let it slide down his gullet until it pooled warm and peaceful in his belly.

"Mighty fine, sir. Thank you. Wish you could partake, too."

"Seeing your enjoyment of it is good enough for me. Now, Mr. Slocum, tell me what happened to Bowden and Thompson."

"I reckon you've already heard," Slocum said slowly. He touched the silver concha in his pocket and decided not to mention it to the mine owner.

"Oh, yes, Mr. Miles has told me, but I wanted to hear the details from someone who was down there."

"Why? Isn't it enough to know that two men died?"

"No, sir, it is not!" flared Haining. "How do we prevent such catastrophes in the future? You're an expert when it comes to handling explosives. What can I do to make it safer for you and the rest of the blasting crew?"

Slocum wasn't sure what to say. He didn't think Thompson's death had been an accident. The more he thought back, the more certain he was that Miles and his two henchmen had been responsible. The noises he had heard when he had gone back to fetch his canteen had been Thompson and Bowden scuffling with the foreman and his cronies. Somehow in the fight, Thompson had grabbed at an attacker's hat and come away with Herk's silver hatband ornament. They had detonated the blast to cover the murders.

That was what he had decided had happened, but he couldn't prove a bit of it. Why had Miles fought with Thompson? If there had been any kind of disagreement, Miles could have just fired Thompson and Bowden. All manner of ideas floated through Slocum's mind. Miles seemed so concerned about someone stealing from the mine that maybe he was looking for a scapegoat, either to protect his job or to protect himself from being arrested. He might be the one stealing and Thompson might have been on the verge of accusing him.

Slocum slumped in the chair. He didn't know enough, even after two weeks at the Low Down, to know what was going on.

"Well, sir, how can safety in the mine be improved?"

Slocum started to speak, but Haining held up his hand.

"Come on in, Lucas," the mine owner called.

Slocum shut his mouth and said nothing more. The foreman stood in the doorway, hand resting on a six-shooter he had strapped to his hip.

"Will you escort Darleen over to York? She wants to see some friends. Be careful. There are road agents galore working that road."

"You don't have to worry on that account, Mr. Haining," Miles said. He stared at Slocum with an unfathomable expression. Slocum felt as if he didn't exist—or maybe he did and was as annoying as a bug crawling along the floor.

"See that you're back before sundown."

Miles nodded and disappeared.

"Now, Mr. Slocum, where were we? Ah, yes, mine safety."

"It'd be safer underground if the miners had any confidence in your foreman."

"What? Lucas Miles is a fine man, knowledgeable, and has run the Low Down like a watch. Why, there's nothing that escapes his notice."

"The men don't like him. Does that matter to you?"

"Oh, bosh," Haining said, his hand fluttering as if he shooed away a fly. "You don't know what you're saying. The men admire and respect Lucas. He came highly recommended and has worked out well."

"He doesn't—"

"I won't hear a word against him, Mr. Slocum. I trust him implicitly. Why, you just heard. I trust Lucas enough to send him along as escort for my wife. I would go with her, but I have so deuced much work to do here. You can't believe how difficult it is paying the bills and keeping a steady flow of matériel into the mine. You're not wanting for anything down below, are you? Of course not. I make sure of that."

"What's the paydirt like?" Slocum asked suddenly. "I haven't seen any of the ore go out that looked as if it had a fleck of gold in it."

"Why, we're drawing better than four ounces a ton. The Low Down is one of the richest mines in the district. It would be richer if it weren't for the outlaws who prey on shipments back to Denver."

An idea occurred to Slocum.

"You lose a lot in shipment?"

"Why, no, not at all. We haven't lost a single ounce in the past six months, because I hire the best guards in the business."

Slocum remembered seeing the riflemen and the guards and driver on the shipment leaving for Denver the first night he had been in town. While it might not have been a shipment from the Low Down, it was well protected.

"You're sure of your assay?"

"Quite, sir. What are you implying?"

"Nothing," Slocum said. "I've got an inventory of explosives I took." He fished it out of his pocket. "We could use another ten kegs of blasting powder if you want to push on through the plug on the lowest level. It's harder rock than it first appeared, but . . ."

"But the quartz content is high. I know. I have personally examined some of the samples. I have been trained as a geologist. That's how I happened upon the Low Down in the first place, when no one else thought it was worth digging."

"You've got a good mine if you're drawing four ounces to the ton of dross," Slocum said. The yield was moderately good, and if they found a richer vein, such as the one Thompson had hoped for, the assay would run far higher. "About those ten kegs."

"Done, Mr. Slocum. And no more of that nonsense about the men not respecting Lucas. He can be a hard taskmaster, but that's why I hired him. I have noticed a tendency of some miners to slack off. I am glad you are not one of that kind. Keep your shoulder to the wheel and you will be both respected and in a position of importance in the mine, not that being head powderman is not an important post."

"Yes, sir, I understand," Slocum said, standing. Haining's thoughts were obviously drifting back to the work spread out on his desk. "Thanks for the whiskey."

"Think nothing of it. And if there are real problems, take them up with Lucas."

Slocum left without another word. Lucas Miles was the last person in the world he would take any concern to. Or to Herk or Singer.

He had started back down the path toward the mine when he noticed a woman near a storage shed watching him intently. Slocum appreciated the way she looked at him, so he tipped his hat in her direction. She was slim, perhaps twenty, dark hair and bright blue eyes with about the prettiest smile he had seen since coming to Colorado. She wore a gingham dress and filled it well.

Slocum intended to pass by, but the woman called out to him.

"Yoohoo, mister, please. Can you come here a minute?" She gestured for him to join her.

"Can I help you, ma'am?"

"Please, call me Evangeline. Evie, to my friends."

"Miss Evangeline," Slocum said. "Pleased to meet you." He introduced himself.

"Then I'll call you John."

Slocum wondered at her insistence on first names.

"John, I couldn't help overhearing what you said to . . . Mr. Haining."

"You eavesdropped?" Slocum considered her hesitation in naming the mine owner. "What was so important that you'd spy on us?"

"It's quite important," she said, her face going blank. He saw how tears began to well up and wondered what was going on. The young woman tried to hide all emotion and only partly succeeded. "You said that there was unrest among the miners. Can you say more about that?"

"No more than you already heard," Slocum said. He didn't like this line of questioning, even if it was pleasant to be in the company of such a lovely filly. Her midnight-dark hair was clean, and she smelled better than anyone he had come across in a month of Sundays. Her face was well scrubbed, but tiny flushed spots showed on her cheeks. Whatever was going through her head caused strong emotions.

"It's most important to me, John. If you could tell me what's happening in the mines, I would be most appreciative." She blushed even more and averted her eyes. The obvious reward she promised further perplexed Slocum. He wasn't averse to spending more time with her, but what she offered in return for gossip seemed out of proportion to what he would get.

"Why? I could tell you anything," he said.

"But you wouldn't. I heard what you said, and you were sincere. The other men matter to you. The mine matters."

"I don't give two hoots about the mine, Miss Evangeline," he said. "I do care about men dying, though. Especially since it might be me buried alive down there. It's dangerous work, and there's no cause to make it more so."

"I wasn't offering my—" Evangeline blushed furiously now. "I didn't mean you could ... we would ... oh!" She turned away, embarrassed.

"I'm sorry if I got the wrong idea, but that's what it sounded like to me. What *is* your interest in the mine? Why not ask Mr. Haining? You seem to know your way around here, and he's an honest man."

"You think so?"

"Yes," Slocum said, "but I also think he's got too many things other than seeing to the daily routine to worry about."

"And you don't think Lucas Miles is capable of dealing with that?"

"You must not, either, or you'd ask Miles," Slocum said.

"Please, John. This is important. Whatever you hear about unrest or thieving or ... anything, please, please let me know."

"I haven't worked at the Low Down very long," Slocum said. "Why do you think you can trust me?"

She turned and looked deep into his green eyes. A smile danced on her lips again, then brightened to a full grin.

"I know." She reached out and brushed her fingertips along his stubbled cheek. Then Evangeline turned and dashed off. Slocum watched as she went down the hill, took a path leading toward Cripple Creek, and eventually disappeared. He heaved a deep sigh. That was one lovely woman, but he had no idea why she was mixed up in this, or what she really wanted from him.

Trudging on back to the Low Down shaft, Slocum bellowed for Billy. The young man got off a powder keg and sauntered over.

"Get two kegs of Giant," Slocum said. "I want to blast that drift open by the end of the shift."

"She really put a bug into your ear, is that it?"

"What did you say?"

"Miss Evangeline. I saw her talkin' with you. She's lookin' mighty fine, considerin'."

"What's it to you that she was talking to me?"

"Nothin', Slocum, nothin' at all."

They walked silently to the elevator, each with a keg of blasting powder on his shoulder. Slocum dropped his to the elevator platform and signaled the operator to lower them to the bottom of the mine. Wood creaking and chains rattling, the elevator began its slow descent.

Only when they were below and the powder had been moved did Slocum turn to Billy.

"You know more of what's going on than I do," Slocum said. "What's Evangeline's interest in the mine?"

"You don't know, do you, Slocum? I'll be damned. You *don't* know!"

Slocum said nothing. He knew Billy would get around to telling him as soon as his enjoyment of the situation died a mite. And he did.

"You don't know what her last name is, do you? It's Haining."

"Evangeline Haining?" Slocum's mind raced. Morgan Haining had asked the foreman to escort his wife, Darleen, to the next town south. "She's the owner's daughter?"

"None other than."

"Certainly explains why she was in a position to spy on Haining," Slocum said. "But she could ask him. Why would she ask me to find out what problems there are in the mine?"

"You really don't know, do you?" This time Billy was more somber. He looked around, then stepped closer and said in a hoarse whisper, "She figures you're a decent sort, having risked your life like you did to save Thompson."

"I tried to save Bowden, too," Slocum pointed out.

"Yeah, but she wasn't sweet on Bowden."

"She and Thompson—?"

"Yep. Rumor had it they were goin' to get hitched, but Thompson never said nothin' 'bout that. A powder monkey marryin' the boss's daughter? Don't know how that woulda set with Haining."

"He didn't know?"

"Don't get me wrong. Mr. Haining's a fine man, but he's got too rosy a view of the world. He ain't never seen the dust and danger down here often enough to get anything else."

Billy hefted the powder keg and started for the end of the drift. Slocum mulled over what Billy had said, then picked up the other powder keg and followed. They had blasting to do.

5

"Think that'll do it, Slocum?" Billy stepped back and aimed his miner's lamp at the five holes they had drilled into the rock and then tamped full of blasting powder.

"Looks like you got too much for the blast."

"Afraid Miles will complain about the wasted money for the powder?"

Slocum began measuring off the waxy black miner's fuse, getting five sections about the length of his arm. He expertly twisted them into a knot, then laced his roll of fuse in. "Get to sticking the ends of the fuses in."

Billy inserted each of the five ends, secured them with mud, then stepped back and saw Slocum already unrolling the main fuse.

"You seem to know what you're doin'," the miner said, but his tone carried enough doubt that Slocum had to laugh.

"I've seen it done this way before. Saves having a long length of fuse on each hole. Main fuse burns down, sets off the shorter ones, makes it more likely all of them will detonate at the same time."

"Suppose so," Billy said. "How far back we goin'?"

"Out of the level," Slocum said. "Make sure everyone's cleared out before I light the fuse."

Slocum stopped in the larger chamber where half a dozen drifts angled off into the mountainside, cut the fuse, and tossed the remaining roll onto the elevator.

"That's not goin' to set well with Miles. He thinks it's a waste of time gettin' all the men out of the level just to blast."

"He's not here and I am. Didn't I get myself promoted to master powderman?"

"Reckon so. How many're workin' this level?"

"Miles told me he had three men besides us working this level, down yonder." Slocum pointed to the drift where he and Billy had been working before the accident with Thompson and Bowden. Or what had been called an accident. Slocum still carried Herk's concha as a reminder.

"Want me to fetch them or let them work?"

"Get them out of here. No reason to risk more men if I did get the amount of powder wrong."

Billy lit out and came back in a few minutes trailing a trio of miners.

"You sure it's all right to break off?" asked one. "Miles don't like it. Says we're lazy if he finds us not swinging a pick or doin' something else productive."

"Destructive," corrected another. "When was the last time we found a gold nugget, much less dust?"

"Get into the elevator," Slocum said. "That all of you down the drift?"

"All," confirmed the first miner.

Slocum pulled out his tin box of lucifers, selected one, then struck it on the rock wall. A flare of sulphur faded down to a steady flame. He applied it to the end of the miner's fuse.

"Got fifteen feet on it. That gives us fifteen minutes to get clear."

"Don't bother me takin' a break," the first miner said, "but you gotta square it with Miles. The man ought to be workin' on a plantation."

"He sure enough thinks we're his slave field hands. Does everything but whip us," said the second.

The elevator began creaking its way up to the next level. When it stopped, Slocum chased the miners out into the small chamber built for the unloading of equipment and men before they dispersed down the spiderweb of tunnels.

"How come you're comin' up and leavin' the others?" asked the elevator operator.

"What others? Miles said there were just the five of us on the lower level."

"Five plus two," the operator said. "Randolph and his kid are down there, too. Least, I took them down early in the shift."

"Before we went down?" Slocum asked.

"Yup."

Slocum muttered under his breath, then said, "Get me back down there. Miles didn't tell me he had sent anyone but us to work that level."

"They can ride out the blast," the operator said, licking his lips nervously. His tongue captured a fair amount of dust and grit that made him spit. "Don't usually evacuate a level to blast."

"We're doing it my way," Slocum said.

"Climb on, then." The operator yanked the bell rope to signal the men at the top that they wanted to lower the elevator. When nothing happened, the operator tugged again. No response.

"What's wrong?"

"Don't know, unless they took their lunch break. It's early for that, but those yahoos are lazy sons of bitches."

Slocum looked up and saw nothing but a tiny dot of light at the head of the shaft. He flopped on his belly and peered down the fifteen feet to the level where he had set the charge.

He shouted at the top of his lungs but got no response. He looked back over his shoulder.

"You sure Randolph and his son are down there?"

"Less they turned into smoke and drifted up this here chimney, they're down there. There ain't a back door."

Cursing a blue streak, Slocum gripped the edge of the elevator platform and slid between it and the rock wall. He lost some skin but hardly noticed. When his feet dangled free, he lowered himself as far as he could, then let loose. He fell and landed hard, but he was ready for the impact. Bones aching, he got to his feet and tried to figure which of the other three drifts Randolph might be working. Pressing his ear to the rock didn't work. He didn't even hear voices. The smell of the burning fuse came to him, but there was plenty of time to get the men to safety. The fuse hadn't even burned down to the five-fold yoke yet.

Dropping to his knees and shining his light on the dusty floor, Slocum found fresh boot prints leading away. With the lack of wind in the mine, these "fresh" prints might have been left a couple days ago, but he had to see.

"Randolph!" he shouted. "Fire in the hole! Get out now! To the elevator!" Slocum craned his neck around and heard the bell ringing furiously. The operator was trying to get the attention of the men manning the winch at the top of the shaft. By the time the platform had been lowered, there'd be scant time to get back to the higher levels.

"Randolph!" The name echoed down the drift, but he heard no response. He shouted down the other drifts but again got no response. The operator might have been wrong. He might have left his elevator to take a piss, and Randolph and his son might have returned to the surface. Slocum didn't think so. In his gut he knew they were still in the mine.

Racing down the drift, bouncing off the rugged walls like some human billiard ball, Slocum finally burst into a large chamber. Randolph and his son pounded away with chisel and hammer. The ringing was muffled by a heavy rag tied to the hammer.

"Randolph," Slocum said, gasping for breath. "We gotta get out." The men kept working.

Slocum went to them and grabbed the younger man's arm to keep him from swinging the heavy sledgehammer. The miner jumped a foot, his eyes wide and frightened.

"We gotta go. Now!"

He frowned, then looked at his pa. The elder Randolph abandoned his grip on the steel bit and came over.

"How's that? We're both a touch hard of hearing."

"Then why'd you muffle the hammer?"

"Keeps down vibration. Don't hurt the joints so bad." Randolph spoke a little too loud, in the manner of a deaf man. "What you want?"

"Fire in the hole," Slocum said, making sure he faced the man so Randolph could read his lips. "We don't have much time to get out of here before the blast goes off."

"We always work through the blasting. Don't hear nuthin', so it don't bother either of us much."

"I'm not taking any chances after what happened to Thompson and Bowden," he said. Slocum grabbed the men by the arms and steered them toward the elevator. He hoped the operator had succeeded in lowering it. Being in the main chamber when the blast went off would be worse than staying down the drift.

"Damn shame what happened to them," Randolph said. His son gestured like an Indian using sign language. His pa responded. "He says he don't want to be docked for takin' time off."

"I'm in charge. Nobody will have their pay docked for the time waiting for the blast."

Slocum neared the chamber where the elevator should have been waiting. He saw that it still hadn't descended. Cursing, he ran to look up the shaft and saw the elevator going up to the surface.

He motioned for the Randolphs to stay put in the mouth of their drift, then ran down his own drift to pull the fuse away from his charges. Slocum hadn't gone five feet when the blast picked him up and threw him backward. He landed hard on his back and skidded, with a rain of dust and rock cascading down on top of him. Slocum sputtered and brushed the debris off his face. He sat up and felt the world spin wildly. His ears had been damaged again, and it would take a few seconds to regain both hearing and balance.

"You two all right?" Slocum shouted. With the ringing so loud in his ears, he knew how the Randolphs felt. Looking back over his shoulder through the brown cloud of roiling dust, Slocum tried to find the two men.

A cold lump formed in his belly when he saw that the mouth of their drift had collapsed. He rolled to hands and knees, then forced himself to his feet. Stumbling forward, he reached the rock fall. The Randolphs had to be trapped behind it—or under it, like Bowden and Thompson.

"Are you alive?" Slocum knew as he shouted it wouldn't do any good. Even if they were alive and uninjured, the men were as deaf as posts. He stepped back, judged what had to be done, then grabbed a pick and began working at the top of the rock fall. Putting his back into it produced immediate results. A small dark hole about the size of Slocum's head appeared to one side.

He tossed down the pickax and clambered up the slope of loose rock and aimed his carbide light though it. The dust was choking thick on the other side but he saw movement.

"Randolph!" He waggled the light back and forth to catch the miner's attention.

"My boy," Randolph said, his face suddenly filling the small opening. "A big rock fell on him. It will crush the breath from his lungs."

"Help me widen the hole," Slocum said.

Randolph dug furiously. Slocum matched him rock for rock and soon had a hole wide enough to wiggle through. He tumbled down the other side and went to the pinned miner. Slocum gestured for Randolph to grab the other side of the large rock. When he had his fingers under the sharp-edged slab, Slocum began lifting. He grunted and his pulse pounded furiously in his temples. He felt veins protruding, but he kept lifting. With a loud shout, he and Randolph moved the rock enough to take the pressure off the son's chest.

A groan was their reward.

Slocum leaned to one side and Randolph followed. They dropped the heavy rock and turned to the injured miner. Slocum saw how hard it was for the young man to breathe. Every time his chest rose, he turned a little whiter under the layer of filth covering his face.

"Busted ribs," Slocum said, gently probing. He looked around and found a couple ax handles. Working deliberately, he strapped them onto the young man's side and down his leg, preventing twisting or much movement in his lower limbs.

"Don't thrash around too much," Slocum said. "Wish we had some whiskey to help you kill the pain, but we don't."

Randolph touched Slocum's arm and pointed to the rock fall, then made digging motions.

"I need to rest first. If there's any mercy in the world, Billy will be back with a crew to do the digging for us," he said. Slocum was tired to the bottoms of his feet. Having done all he could for the younger Randolph, he needed to rest a few minutes.

Randolph sank beside him but kept a close watch on his son.

"You risked your life," Randolph said. His speech was curiously slurred. Slocum reckoned that he and maybe his son had been born deaf. Or partially deaf. "Thank you."

"My own fault for not checking better before I lit the fuse, but Miles didn't tell me he had sent you down here, too."

"He will be unhappy," Randolph said.

"From what I can tell, Miles is always unhappy about something."

Randolph looked at him curiously.

"What?" Slocum asked.

"You have not heard why? High-graders."

"People stealing from the mine?" Slocum knew that might have been why Miles and his henchmen had tried to search Bowden, Billy, Thompson, and himself before Bowden and Thompson died. It wasn't out of spite but real need to maintain security. What Slocum could fault the foreman for was not choosing better whom to search. None of them was the kind to steal—or had been.

"They try to find out but they cannot discover how it is done. A new vein is found and it peters out fast."

"That's bad luck."

"It has been mined," Randolph said. "We open new chambers and find gold already gone. How this is possible, I do not know. No one does." Randolph shrugged his massive shoulders.

Slocum turned when he heard the rattle of pebbles. He directed his light toward the small hole he had used to reach the Randolphs and saw Billy poking his head through.

"You gents are still alive. Fancy that," the young miner said.

"One's real bad off. Ribs broken. Doesn't look as if a bone has punctured a lung, though." Slocum had watched the younger Randolph's mouth and nose for any trace of pink froth showing a lung had been breached, but other than a nasty wheezing sound, nothing else came out.

"Won't take us a minute to get through. Got half the crew here."

"Why'd the elevator go up?"

"Damn fool atop is brand-new and got screwed up on the signals. He thought he was supposed to raise, not lower. But no harm, eh?"

In less than ten minutes the miners had reopened the drift and worked in new timbers to hold the roof. Randolph and his son left, taken to the surface to find a doctor to patch up the busted ribs. Slocum knew a plaster patch would let the young man get back to work in a day or two. Depending on how much they needed the money, he might be back to work tomorrow.

"I want to see if the blast did anything more than almost kill me," Slocum said. "The fuse burned a hell of a lot faster than I thought it would."

"Might have been defective." Billy looked at Slocum and shrugged as he held out his hands, palms up in apology. "It happens. Mr. Haining's not always buyin' from the best suppliers."

"Cheap gets you killed," muttered Slocum as he picked his way through the rubble to where he and Billy had planted the five charges. The dust had settled enough for him to examine their handiwork.

"This is one fine job of blastin', Slocum. Thompson couldn't have done better." Billy picked up a rock the size of his fist and examined it closely. "Glory be, this is gold! We hit the vein we lost a couple weeks back."

Slocum noted how uniformly the rock had been blasted. He had wondered if he had the touch to do that. The muckers would come in and shovel the rock into a skip car much more easily since they didn't have to break up the rock further.

More than fifteen feet of new tunnel had been blasted. Slocum picked up a few chunks and examined them. He had a good eye for color. Gold. Plenty of it. There were even a few small nuggets the size of the tip of his little finger among the larger rocks.

"This ought to keep the Low Down in the black for a spell," Slocum said, pleased at how well this had worked out.

He looked up when he heard boots approaching. Turning his head a mite sprayed light across Lucas Miles's ugly face. Behind him came Herk and Singer. Neither of the henchmen looked at all pleased.

"What do you mean sendin' my miners up while you work?" Miles demanded. "They put in a full day's work or they get docked!"

"It was dangerous blasting here. The drifts haven't been properly shored."

"One collapsed. So?"

"So that was the one where Randolph and his son were working. I tried to get them out before the powder went off, but I didn't make it."

"You were lollygaggin', too. I'm dockin' yer pay a full shift, Slocum."

"Even when he just made Mr. Haining a small fortune? Might not be a big fortune, but it's surely a good one." Billy juggled three rocks and then tossed them to Miles and his two cronies. Miles and Herk caught theirs. Singer fumbled and dropped his.

"Take a good look, Miles," Slocum said. "I'm not an expert, but assay ought to show that'll yield forty or fifty ounces a ton. Might be more."

"More," Billy assured him.

"Them rocks look mighty uniform in size, boss," said Herk. "That's the mark of a good blaster."

"Shut up," snapped Miles. "You aren't foreman. If I want men workin', they will damn well work! Do you understand, Slocum?"

"Yeah," Slocum said. "I understand."

"See that you do. I don't give a pair of bull's balls how good you are, you cross me, you counter my orders, and you're fired."

"Might be worth leaving' anyway," Billy said.

"What do you mean?"

"Mr. Haining said we get a bonus for exceeding quotas, finding more gold—"

"Shut up. *I* pass out the bonuses, and I don't see nuthin' other than the usual ore. All worthless rock."

"Then you won't mind if I put a few chunks of this 'worthless' ore into my pocket for a keepsake?" Billy laughed when Miles swept his paw of a hand through the air and knocked the gold-bearing rocks back onto the pile.

"Don't go pushin' me, boy."

"Just wonderin' how it is," Billy said, squaring his shoulders and almost bumping chests with the taller, heavier Lucas Miles. "Is it worthless or do we get a bonus? Has to be one way or the other. Fact is, I hope you tell me it's worthless. I've taken a real fancy to the rocks Slocum blasted free for you."

The foreman growled and pushed Billy away. He spun and stalked off, Herk and Singer following at his heels.

"You're playing a dangerous game. Never pays to bait a grizzly like that," said Slocum.

"If you can't get rich in this life, why not have a little

fun?" Billy said. He picked up the rock and stared at it. "Sure as hell ain't us gettin' rich, but I'm glad Mr. Haining is."

From what Randolph had told him, Slocum wasn't sure Morgan Haining was seeing a fraction of what was mined in the Low Down.

6

Slocum left the mine feeling tired but good that he had blasted open a new vein that might bring the Low Down back into profitability. The idea that he and the rest of the miners would get a bonus wasn't too bad, either. He hadn't been around that many mines, but the notion that the owner thought so highly of his workers that he gave such a lagniappe made Slocum feel that Lady Luck had smiled on him when he got the job.

"Slocum," came a gruff voice. He turned and saw Randolph and his son. "You have found new vein, eh?"

"Seemed to. Hunks of rock are on their way to the assay office to see how good it is."

"We had vein before but it petered out. You found it. You make us all money!" Randolph slapped him on the back. "I buy you drinks!"

"Done," Slocum said, grinning. "Let me get to the bunkhouse first."

Randolph was already heading for other miners to tell them what had happened. The Low Down was a profitable mine again. Word spread fast. Slocum began making his way up the hill to the run-down bunkhouse when he saw Lucas Miles almost running along a path in the direction of the mine's main office. He slowed and then watched as

Evangeline Haining came into view. From his vantage it looked the world like Miles was laying an ambush for the woman.

When she saw the mine foreman, she stopped and the set to her body changed. She had been intent on her errand and hadn't noticed him until she almost ran into him. Slocum was too far away to hear, so he changed his own path and worked higher on the hill, trying not to be too obvious about eavesdropping. The rugged hillside worked in his favor and he got within a dozen paces.

From a distance it looked as if they were swapping pleasantries. Closer, Slocum heard what was being said.

"I have no interest in that, Mr. Miles." Evangeline crossed her arms and rocked back, looking at him down her button nose. Try as she might, she couldn't look ferocious, but she made an effort.

"Why not? I run the mine. I just struck a new vein of gold that'll make your pa even richer. You could do worse than take up with me."

"No."

"Still carryin' a torch for Thompson? Is that it?" Miles stepped closer, forcing Evangeline to back off. "Let me tell you something, missy. He's dead. He ain't comin' back. Ever."

"I'm still in mourning for him, sir." Evangeline began looking around, as if she wanted to bolt and run. Something in the woman caused her to stand her ground, in spite of Miles's rubbing up against her now.

"Let me help you forget him. It'll be real nice for both of us. I promise." He reached out to touch her cheek. Evangeline batted his hand away, then shoved him hard to get him at a more civil distance. She wasn't strong enough to move him.

"Stop!" Evangeline yelped when Miles grabbed her arms and pulled her in close for a kiss. Slocum reached for his six-gun, then remembered it was with the rest of his gear. He started to get around the boulder where he eavesdropped, then stopped.

Evangeline had stepped closer, letting Miles think she

was yielding to him. Instead, she got close enough to raise her knee into his groin with enough power to cause him to grunt.

When he didn't let go, she kneed him again. This time he stumbled back, giving her room to her kick out and connect with his knee. Trying to hold his crotch, with his knee gone out from under him, he fell to the dirt path.

"You bitch," he snarled. "You'll be sorry. I—"

"You overstep your bounds, Mr. Miles." She was flushed and stood with her hands balled into fists. "I'll have my papa fire you for this!"

"He won't believe you. He'll think you made a play for me. You'll only get yourself into trouble."

"You're the only trouble I need to get rid of, sir!" she flared.

Slocum thought she looked downright pretty. Her cheeks were flushed and her chin was set. Her shoulders were back and she looked as if she would go ten rounds with Miles in a bare-knuckles fight if need be. But Slocum would never allow it to come to that. He started around the boulder again, but Miles had already backed off. He muttered curses as he hobbled away, still clutching where Evangeline had kicked him.

Evangeline swung about, her fists coming up as Slocum skidded down the hillside. She relaxed a little when she saw who it was.

"Whoa," Slocum said. "I don't mean no harm. I thought you might need some help, but you handled yourself mighty well."

Evangeline lowered her hands and self-consciously smoothed nonexistent wrinkles from her gingham dress. She smiled wanly, looked in Miles's direction, then back at Slocum.

"Why, John, I do believe you *were* coming to my aid. How gallant of you."

"Not so gallant," Slocum said. "I saw Miles hightail it down the path, spotted you, and then I decided I ought to eavesdrop."

"Indeed," Evangeline said, but she sounded more intrigued than outraged at his behavior. "And why do you think you ought to spy on me?"

"Not on you. Him." Slocum jerked his thumb in the direction taken by the mine foreman. "He's meaner than a stepped-on sidewinder."

"He's Papa's foreman," she said.

"That doesn't make him any more likable."

"I wish you were foreman," Evangeline said suddenly.

"Or Thompson?"

"Yes, or Tommy. He was a good man." She fixed her bright blue eyes on him. "You have been nosing about, haven't you, John?"

"Not much else to do down in a mine other than swing a pick, breathe dust, and gossip."

"Somehow, I never thought of miners as a bunch of old women at a sewing bee," she said. "Is that really what you talk about? My love life?"

"Why not? You're about the prettiest woman in Cripple Creek. There's got to be some speculation about you and whoever you're courting."

"Like Mr. Thompson?"

"The name did crop up," Slocum said.

"Have you come to report on the matter I asked about, or were you only spying on me?"

"Does it matter?"

For a moment Evangeline was taken aback. Then she laughed.

"You are quite assured of yourself, aren't you?"

"No reason to doubt myself," Slocum said. "And I haven't heard anything worth passing along about conditions in the mine, other than that there was a big strike today."

"You *are* modest, aren't you, John? Who might it have been who blasted into a vein ten feet wide with a two-foot spread? Color in all the rock. The assayist says it might prove out better than thirty ounces to the ton."

"You are remarkably well informed."

"Perhaps I have taken an interest in you, as you seem to have in me."

"Your well-being," Slocum said, "looked to be compromised by Miles. I was only doing what any man would."

"Spying on me?" Evangeline brushed back vagrant strands of her raven-dark hair, then moved her hands slowly across the top button on her dress. Slocum never saw how she unbuttoned it and showed just a tad more skin, but she did.

"I can think of worse people to set and watch," Slocum said.

"Then please join me for some tea. I have a fresh pot brewed only this morning."

"Tea? I had some once. A British remittance man wouldn't drink anything else until I rescued him by giving him some boiled trail coffee. After that he never touched tea again."

"I can always prepare some coffee, if you prefer something stronger."

"It doesn't matter," Slocum said. "But would it be proper, you inviting me like this?"

"Of course it is. Papa and Mama are home. What impropriety could there be?"

Slocum laughed. When she joined him, he knew the same sort of impropriety was going through the lovely woman's head as his. He dusted himself off a mite and then caught up with her.

"Where's your house?"

"On the far side of the hill where the office is located," she said. "See? We just take that path around the base and we'll be there."

Slocum knew this was wrong. He had a thought he might tarnish the woman's reputation if anyone saw them together, then pushed it out of his mind. She'd said her pa was home. Anyone seeing them would think they were going to see Morgan Haining and nothing more. He hoped. Slocum had taken quite a liking to Evangeline and didn't want to do anything that would besmirch her standing in the community. All boomtowns were flush with two things: whiskey and gossip.

The house was a modest one for a rich mine owner, but it fit with what Slocum thought about Morgan Haining—and his daughter. They were less inclined to flaunt their wealth than they were to use it for good. Slocum wondered what would be his share of the bonus for finding the gold vein—and a rich one at that, if the report from the assayist was accurate.

"Hello!" she called. "Hello, anyone home?"

Slocum hesitated at the doorstep. He listened hard for any sound in the house and heard nothing but the wood slowly settling.

"Maybe I had better go," he said. "It doesn't look as if either of your folks is home."

"Nonsense," Evangeline said firmly. "I promised you tea—or coffee—and you shall get it. Moreover, I want to hear what you have heard in the mine. Other than about me."

"Other?" Slocum grinned.

Evangeline grinned back and added, "Perhaps after you have told me other news, then you can tell what the men think of me."

"Might not be to your liking. Miners can be a mite crude."

"I won't mind . . . if *you* tell me." Before he could say a word, she swung about, her skirts lifting high and showing an indecent amount of ankle and calf as she hurried from the parlor to the kitchen.

"Oh, good," she said. "There's already coffee on the stove."

Slocum stood and shuffled his feet. He didn't want to sit in any of the chairs because he would leave a patch of dust behind. After a long shift of blasting and digging furiously with a pickax, he was covered with fine rock dust. Even standing stock-still where he was left a small pile of soft white dust on the floor around his feet.

He looked up when Evangeline returned. His eyes went a little wider because she had contrived to open three more buttons on her dress, giving him a delectable sight. The swell of her snowy white breasts bounced slightly as she moved. The dark-haired woman took no notice that her dress was coming undone, but Slocum couldn't take his eyes off her.

"Sugar?" she asked.

"Black is fine. Black like your hair," he said, moving forward. As she put the coffee down on a table, he reached out and slid his fingers through her silken hair. It flowed like water beneath his touch until his palm came to rest behind her head. They looked at each other for an instant, then Evangeline's eyes half closed. Slocum kissed her. Or did she kiss him? The ardor in their kiss mounted until he was gasping for breath.

"I shouldn't do this," he said.

"No, you shouldn't. Neither should I," the woman said. She pushed him back a step. His heart hammered in his chest and his pants were getting uncomfortably tight, but he knew what was right. He had to leave.

But he didn't.

He was frozen to the spot, watching Evangeline as she finished unbuttoning her dress until it hung open to the waist. She twisted this way and that, shrugged her shoulders, and got out of the obscuring fabric so that it hung about her hips. Then she was naked to the waist.

Slocum licked his lips as he stared at her firm, apple-sized breasts. They were capped with bright pink nubs that grew visibly harder as he watched.

"It's hard to hide what you feel, isn't it?" she said in a husky voice.

"I see something that I want," he said, reaching out to cup her tits. His fingers curled around those throbbing nubs and produced a small gasp. She stepped forward, crushing herself into his big hands. He tweaked those nips, twisting and turning them until he felt the beating of her heart through them.

"Oh, John, yes. I want you so!"

He stopped the torrent of words in the most delightful

way possible. He kissed her hard. She melted against him, her bare chest mashing against his filthy clothing. But this was only a problem for a few seconds. Her nimble, knowing fingers worked to get him naked to the waist, too. Then bare flesh pressed into equally bare, warm flesh.

They turned around and around in one another's arms, as if dancing to silent music.

Somehow Slocum got out of his boots and Evangeline got his pants pulled down so he could kick free of the dirty rags. Then those dancing fingers of hers curled around his hardness and gently squeezed down until he moaned in pleasure.

"You like that?"

"Yes," he said.

"Then you'll like this even more." Her hands went around his back and boldly slid down to his muscular rump. She sank slowly to her knees, kissing his chest and belly as she went. When she was on her knees, she pulled on the double handful of muscled ass and drew his crotch forward. His meaty shaft slid easily, willingly, wantonly between her lips. Slocum felt his knees turn weak with desire when she began licking and tonguing his fierce length. After a few seconds he couldn't restrain himself. His hips began thrusting forward, driving his fleshy spike farther into her mouth.

She took him. Every inch. And her tongue slipped under the sensitive head to give him even more stimulation. He ran his fingers through her hair once more, lacing through the strands so he could pull and push her in the rhythm that excited him most.

But after several minutes, he withdrew. There was a wet *pop!* as he slid free of her mouth. She looked up questioningly.

"More," he said. "I want to give you more."

Before she could say a word, he reached down and his strong hands lifted her entirely off the floor. Swinging her around, her placed her on the table. Her legs spread under her dress, but the target he aimed for was still hidden. With a sweeping motion he pushed aside the obscuring cloth and viewed paradise. Tiny dewdrops dotted the tangled nest hidden between her strong thighs.

Slocum stroked over the fleecy hair and inserted his finger. This brought the first real gasp of desire from Evangeline's lips. Her body quaked as he continued to slip in and out of her heated core. His hand came away oily with her inner juices. Then he stepped up.

Hands going under her knees, he lifted fast and moved forward in a smooth motion. He sank into the depths of her channel. Suddenly surrounded by clinging, hot female flesh, he was forced to hesitate. His iron control almost disappeared like a young buck out for action the first time. Slocum swallowed hard, looked down into Evangeline's passion-racked face, and saw the way her breasts heaved up and down. She tensed all around him, and he could no longer stand to simply wait.

He drew back until only the purpled arrowhead of his manhood remained within her. Then he pistoned forward, sinking balls-deep into her. She groaned in desire. Her knees drew up double as her legs parted even more for him.

"Yes, John, oh, I need this, I need it so bad!"

He needed it, also. It had been too long for him and seldom had he ever seen such a willing, lovely filly. Slocum began moving with long, slow movements, taking his time, building both their desires to the breaking point.

When Evangeline gasped, arched her back, and clamped down fiercely all around him with her strong inner muscles, he had to fight to keep from spurting out his load. Reaching down, he gripped her fleshy buttocks and pulled her powerfully into his groin. He sank an added inch into her clinging inner warmth.

And then the fiery tide rising within his loins could not be denied. He shortened his stroke and moved faster, ever faster, so fast the friction burned along his length and released within her yet another climax.

This time when her female sheath crushed down all

around him, he was unable to resist. He cried out and jammed himself as deeply into her as possible. The hot flow of lava from deep within expanded, slowly at first and then with a potent rush that took away both their breaths.

Only after he was spent did Slocum open his eyes and look down at her. A devilish smile danced on her lips.

"That was more than I expected," she said softly. "Ever so much more. Thank you."

"Any time you want to start again, let me know."

Evangeline sat up and reached for his increasingly limp shaft. She stroked it, but he pried her fingers off.

"Not now. You could wear a man out."

"Oh, you could wear down an inch or two and still be mighty fine, John," she said.

"We'd better get dressed. It wouldn't do to have your pa or ma see us like this."

"I doubt either would see anything they haven't seen before."

"I like my job. I don't want to get fired—or worse. Your pa struck me as a man of great honor. If he didn't challenge me to a duel, he would probably just shoot me outright."

Evangeline laughed, but she hopped off the table and pushed down her skirt before slipping back into the top of her dress and buttoning herself up.

Slocum was torn between watching all that creamy skin vanish back behind its veil of gingham and getting dressed himself. But he managed to climb back into his pants, get his boots on, and then finish putting on his shirt about the same time Evangeline was decent again.

"Now," she said almost primly. "Coffee?" She poured a healthy dollop into a cup.

Slocum could hardly believe this was the woman he had just shared such an intimate moment with. She was the perfect hostess as she held out a china cup on a saucer for him.

"Thanks."

"You said black. Are you sure? I have both cream and sugar."

"Oh, I got plenty of sugar," he said. This produced a little blush that extended from her face to the base of her throat and downward. He imagined what it looked like covering the tops of her breasts.

"We should discuss some business," Evangeline said. She sat on the edge of a chair, her cup and saucer balanced delicately.

"Business?"

"How are we going to stop the high-graders stealing from my papa's mine?"

7

Slocum left the Haining house feeling a curious mixture of elation and caution. It was as if he had found some man's cheating wife, but being with Evangeline was nothing like that. She wasn't married. And she sure was willing. It still felt as if he had done something wrong. Maybe it was her recent wooing by Thompson or that she was the mine owner's daughter. Slocum couldn't figure what it was that made him so uneasy.

He returned to the bunkhouse fighting the sensation that someone watched his every step. More than once Slocum stopped and carefully looked around but saw no one. Shrugging it off as nothing more than nerves, he shucked off his clothes—again—and switched to cleaner ones. Then he headed out to the main street running the length of Cripple Creek to find where Randolph and the rest of the miners from the Low Down had gone.

It didn't take a man as skilled as he was in tracking to find them. The raucous singing and the sudden appearance of Randolph's son Ira being thrown out into the street showed him the way. Slocum grabbed the young man's collar and pulled him to his feet. Ira was already more than half past drunk.

"You want to sit this one out?" Slocum asked, making certain the miner could read his lips.

"Naw, wanna drink more," Ira Randolph said.

Slocum kept his grip on the greasy collar to steady Ira as he steered him back to the saloon. If the barkeep had tossed Ira out, Slocum would have left him on the boardwalk, but another miner had done the deed. And then gone back to the bar and gotten into a fight with Billy. A single punch had decked him.

Billy rubbed his knuckles, grinned, and waved to Slocum.

"There he is, men. The fella what earned us a big bonus!"

Sudden silence fell in the saloon. Slocum almost backed away when he realized everyone stared at him. Then a loud cheer ripped from the throats of everyone inside.

"I'm buyin'," the elder Randolph said. "I say so, I do it."

Slocum was caught up in the crush that carried him to the bar. A full bottle of rye whiskey clicked onto the bar in front of him, but Slocum was lucky to get a single shot. Too many hands grabbed for the bottle, either to pour into their own glasses or to take a deep draft without benefit of a shot glass.

"Has it been made official?" Slocum asked. "That the vein's good?"

"It's good," said Billy. "I seen the assay report from the chemist. Old Hillman might be blind as a bat but he knows his ore. He said it was 'bout the best damn strike made in Cripple Creek this year."

More bottles were passed up and down the bar, but Slocum drank sparingly. He studied the men gathered to celebrate the new strike and wondered which of them would steal from Morgan Haining. No one looked the least bit shifty. Then he decided even a high-grader might be rejoicing. It meant that much more gold to steal without doing the work needed to find it in the first place.

"Randolph," Slocum said, taking the huge man's arm and steering him toward a corner of the saloon. It wasn't any quieter, but it gave a sense of privacy not afforded by remaining at the long mahogany bar.

"You want somethin'?"

"Advice. You've been a miner for a long time, haven't you?"

"All my life. Well, from when I was half Ira's size. Might be ten years old."

"You mentioned high-graders working the Low Down. How?"

"How?"

"How would a high-grader get the gold out of the mine? I've seen the way gold is guarded around here. It'd take a company of cavalry troopers to pry it loose. If there's high-grading going on, the gold's stolen some other way."

"From the mine, they take ore. Perhaps not all is sent to the mill," Randolph said slowly.

"You mean we dig out the vein, then the ore is hijacked?"

"Perhaps we are not the ones who dig it out. Others go into the mine, maybe, and steal only the best ore. All in Cripple Creek know of Mr. Haining's luck this day."

"So high-graders would be more likely to go to work now than earlier? Before the find?" Slocum scratched his head. For the life of him, he couldn't see how anyone could get ore out of a mine, since it had to be taken up the elevator. The elevator operator changed often so one man couldn't be looking the other way. Could that many men be in on it? Slocum somehow thought one would spill the beans. He didn't know any of the elevator operators who wasn't waiting for a chance to get down into the mines and work, since the pay was more than double. If an operator were getting paid off, he wouldn't be so eager to descend into the dangerous tunnels and breathe dust for ten hours a day.

Randolph shrugged, then lifted his empty glass to let Slocum know that he needed more than talk right now. The partially deaf miner returned to the bar, used his hip to knock another man out of the way, and then pulled his son up and draped him over the broad expanse. Ira started to slip back, but other miners caught him and hoisted him up so he lay flat. The partying went on without Slocum.

He settled down when a chair in the corner came empty, and watched the miners. He shared their elation at the gold find, but he couldn't join in. He preferred a more solitary existence.

Except for times with a woman as fine as Evangeline Haining, he thought, smiling at the memory of being with her. Drink after drink went down his gullet, and then the barkeep threw them all out. Slocum was only a little surprised to see the false dawn outlining the mountains to the east.

It was going to be one hell of a long day down in the mines.

"You ever use that stuff before, Slocum?" Lucas Miles looked edgy as he stared at the glass bottle on the keg between him and Slocum. Both Singer and Herk had already left the shed.

"Nitroglycerin? Some. Why do you need so much power?" He eyed the clear, thick liquid in the bottle. Heat it, it would blow. Drop it, there'd be a crater ten feet across to fill. If that happened, both he and Miles would share the same grave.

"Geologist says the new drift has some real heavy rock in it. You need to use this, since regular blastin' powder's not enough. Otherwise, it'd be like a bird peckin' away. That'd mean a lot of work for not much reward."

"You could always drill more holes and use more black powder," Slocum suggested.

"Takes too long. This is the way the boss wants to go."

"When do we get the bonus from the find yesterday?"

"Next payday. Friday." Miles glared at him, as if it might make him forget and let the foreman keep the bonus money. "You thinkin' of movin' on?"

"Not till I finish blasting with that," Slocum said, pointing to the deadly bottle. "You got a clean funnel and some tubing? If so much as a speck of dirt gets into it, it might blow."

"You gonna drill a hole, then pour it in?"

"That's the way it's done. The holes have to be driven so they slope downward. Otherwise it's too hard to get the nitro in and seal the hole before it drips back out."

"Touch the dirt floor and blooey," Miles said, a touch of awe in his voice. "Never seen what this shit can do."

Slocum hesitated. Why was Miles the foreman if he hadn't used every conceivable tool, every type of explosive? He started to ask what experience Miles had when the shed door opened and Billy stuck his head in.

"You ready to bring down a mountain, Slocum?"

"Reckon so," Slocum said. "The sooner we use this, the sooner it's no longer a danger to us."

"What happens to Slocum's share if he blows himself to kingdom come?" Billy asked. "Can I claim it?"

"Go to hell," Miles grumbled. "And be damn careful movin' that."

"Got a crate filled with sawdust to take up the shock?"

"I'll get one," Billy said, disappearing.

"You coming down to supervise?" Slocum asked, knowing the answer. He liked to see Miles squirm. The foreman did not disappoint him.

"I got to go over to York."

"With Mrs. Haining?" Slocum wasn't sure why he said that, but the expression on the foreman's face flowed from shock to anger and then to a caginess he had seen on tinhorn gamblers when they were getting ready to deal from the bottom of the deck.

"Yeah, somethin' like that. Get on down into the hole. I want production, not jawing."

Miles skirted the keg where the nitro rested, looking as innocent as a new spring day. Barely had the foreman left when Billy returned, carrying a crate stuffed with sawdust.

"This'll do, won't it, Slocum? I couldn't find a bigger one."

"It'll do," Slocum said. He carefully picked up the bottle, then found a funnel and some rubber tubing. "Clean those out real good," Slocum told Billy. "Not a speck of dirt."

"I know," the miner said. "I'll have them spick-and-span by the time you're over at the elevator."

Slocum situated the bottle in the center of the sawdust and then gingerly picked up the crate. With deliberate steps, he made his way the hundred yards to the elevator. He was sure an hour had passed. He had certainly sweat gallons by the time he climbed onto the rickety platform.

"Got the funnel and hose, Slocum," Billy said, running up. "Let's go blow open a new vein!"

He climbed onto the platform but before it started to clang its way down to the lower levels, Miles shouted to him.

"Billy, git yer ass over here. I told you not to do this again."

"What'd I do now? Or not do? Damnation. You gonna wait, Slocum?"

"I'll go on. Catch up with me."

Slocum held his breath all the way down into the mine. He had ordered everyone out of the level where he was going to blast. His carbide lamp cast a ghostly blue light as he followed the drift as it snaked around for what seemed a mile. He finally reached the end of the tunnel. Two long chisels and a sledgehammer rested against the wall he was supposed to blast.

He put down the crate and examined the wall. The rock didn't appear any thicker or tougher than the rest of the mountain. And the geologist hadn't bothered marking where the holes were to be drilled. Slocum peered closely at the rock to find the right spots himself while he waited for Billy.

It seemed an eternity before he straightened and rubbed his sore back. Where was Billy?

Just as he was deciding to go back to find his assistant, he heard a quick shuffle of boots along the drift.

"Hurry it up, will you, Billy?" he called.

The sounds stopped suddenly. Slocum frowned, wondering what Billy was up to. A noise like sawing echoed down the drift. He had started back down the tunnel to find out what was going on when the explosion staggered him.

He slammed hard into the wall he was supposed to blow into rubble and sank down. He sat on the floor, stunned and choking on the dust billowing toward him.

Several seconds later, Slocum took off his bandanna and wiped his face clear of grit. He spat and wished he hadn't left his canteen back in the larger chamber just off the elevator. He spat again, squinted, and began crawling forward to see what had happened. Everything had taken place so quickly he wasn't sure if Billy was hurt—or if he himself was. Slocum stopped to check himself. Other than a few cuts from flying stones, he was unhurt.

Shining his lamp into the thick cloud of dust, he saw that a support beam had collapsed.

"Collapsed, like hell," he muttered to himself. He ran his fingers over the exposed timber that had helped support the now-fallen roof. "Sawed clean through." Slocum cursed himself for not being quicker to investigate the strange sounds. Someone had worked diligently to saw through the beam and cause the cave-in, trapping him. When the roof collapsed, it had sounded like an explosion.

"Can't take too much work to get through the fall," he said, shining his light all over the rock plug in the drift. "Shouldn't take longer than an hour or two, and if Billy's on the other side, a crew will get through in only a few minutes."

As he spoke aloud, a cold knot formed in his belly. He didn't believe Billy had been responsible for trapping him like this. Not for an instant. But someone had gone to a lot of trouble to make it appear to be an accident. That same owlhoot might also have arranged for an "accident" to befall Billy.

Slocum got to work with new determination, throwing rocks back. After several minutes, he stopped to take a break. The air was still good. A sizable segment of the drift had been cut off. He mopped his face with his bandanna, wrung it out, and then wondered if he had scratched his face. It was wetter after he had dried it off than it had been before.

He held out the bandanna and looked at it. No blood. He turned and got a spray of water in the face that forced him to backtrack a few steps.

"Son of a bitch!" Slocum looked around, his light jumping with furious movement. Half the wall near the sawed timber support was wet from a steady stream pouring in from the top. The collapse had weakened the stone and allowed water to come in, whether from an underground river or some trapped subterranean pocket he couldn't tell. And it didn't matter. If there was enough water, it would eventually flood the pocket where he was trapped and he would drown.

Slocum held down his growing panic and backed away to better assess his problems. He hadn't made much of a dent in getting through the plug of rock that blocked his way back to the elevator. And no sounds of digging came through from the other side, although there couldn't be more than five or six feet of obstruction.

He futilely put his hands against the rock wall and tried to find where the water poured in. If he could block the crack, he might stave off disaster. But the crack ran the length of the wall and beyond the rock plug. Even if he had plaster all mixed and ready to apply, stopping the flow was impossible. It was coming from too wide an area.

Backing away, he slipped in the mud forming on the floor. The water level was already midway up his boots. Sloshing around, he worked his way back to the end of the drift, thinking the collapse might show some other way out of the trap he found himself in. It didn't. The crack had opened up only wide enough to allow the water in.

To fill his little pocket of safety.

Slocum would drown within a very short while since the water poured in faster now. His boots were shipping water, and before much longer he would be waist deep.

"Help! Water's pouring in!" he shouted. His words echoed in the ever-smaller chamber and taunted him. No sounds of rescue came from the other side of the rock fall.

Panic overtook him when he realized this was going to be his grave. He was buried alive. That thought made the air a bit stuffier and breathing harder. His chest rose and fell heavily, and his hands shook as he clawed at the rock in a fruitless attempt to pull down enough stone to open a channel out. If he succeeded, the water would flow out and he would be saved.

Slocum panicked even more when he realized that the water probably flooded the other side of the rocky barrier, too. He might open a small channel only to find even more water.

"Don't," he told himself. "Stop it. This is only getting you riled. Calm down. You won't get out of this alive if you don't start thinking straight."

Slocum sucked in a deep breath, and the air wasn't too bad. Stale, yes, but still breathable. He worked his way through thigh-deep water back to pick up a steel chisel and the sledgehammer. He stared at them, wondering what he might do with them. Then a desperate plan came to him. He had no idea how thick the mountain was, but he could extend the chamber a few yards if he blasted. Using the nitro on the rock fall would only get him in a worse predicament. The falling roof had opened an underground stream along one wall. He had to go away from it, maybe blast his way upward to the next higher level from where he was. From there he could get back to the elevator and get the hell out of the Low Down Mine.

Bracing the long chisel with rocks, he clumsily began hammering a hole near the top of the wall. He wanted to blast upward but had to drill the hole downward to hold the nitro. By the time he had several inches of hole, the water was up around his chest. Slocum couldn't work any longer. He had to blast. Now.

He took a deep breath, then plunged underwater to find the funnel and tube. When he surfaced, he saw that the tube had been cut by a flying rock and was useless. He had to use only the funnel. And he had to be mighty careful pouring the nitroglycerin, because the water might set it off.

Sweating even as he worked in the deep water, he got

the funnel slipped into place in the hole he had drilled. Slocum began worrying that the hole wasn't deep enough to make a difference. Then he concentrated entirely on getting the cork out of the nitro bottle and pouring the thick liquid into the broad mouth of the funnel.

Slocum chewed his tongue as he poured. And poured and poured. He began to wonder where the explosive went. The hole hadn't been that deep. Or had it? He couldn't remember how far he had hammered. All he knew was that most of the bottle had been emptied. When he saw a tiny pool at the bottom of the funnel, he stopped pouring and corked the bottle.

"Here goes nothing," he said. Slocum fumbled in his pocket and found the long piece of black miner's fuse he had intended to use. He had brought enough for a ten-minute burn. He bit off only a foot and affixed it to the funnel. Then he lit the other end. The fuse fell down under water for a moment, but that didn't extinguish it. The magnesium center burned brightly, sputtering and sending up a small cloud of steam as it worked its way out of the water and toward the nitro.

Slocum splashed furiously and then swam to get away from the blast site.

The explosion doubled him up and slammed him into the rocky wall. He felt sharp edges cutting into him, and then there was a curious lack of pain.

He felt himself being swept toward the spot where he had blasted, and then let out a scream as the floor fell away under him, sending him plunging downward faster and faster.

8

The sudden rush of water carried Slocum into darkness and battered him about like a woodchip in a millrace. As quickly as the water had grabbed him, it was gone. He lay facedown in mud, panting harshly and wondering if this was what it was like being dead. He hoped not. He hurt all over. To spend an eternity with aches, pains, and cuts would be a real hell.

Forcing himself to hands and knees, he looked around. Surprisingly, his carbide lamp still worked. He reached up and adjusted it to shine directly in front of him. The tunnel looked different. Then he turned over and sat heavily. Behind him ran a steady stream of water from above. He peered up and around and saw what had happened. Although he had blasted at the top of the drift, hoping to reach the level above where he had been trapped, the bottom had fallen out of the shaft and sent him downward. Into another tunnel.

The water poured like a waterfall and vanished into holes at the end of this tunnel, disappearing back into the underground river. He didn't try to figure out what this all meant, other than that he wasn't dead. Being safe and relatively intact was all that mattered.

Going back to the spot where he had blasted through, he

saw he had fallen about ten feet. The new tunnel ran at an angle to the drift above, and he knew this one hadn't been blasted by anyone working for the Low Down Mine. He had been on the lowest level, and this one was even deeper. It meandered around and headed back toward the spot where he imagined the vein he had unearthed the day before must dive down. Bending over, he directed his light onto the wall. The vein had to have dipped down, like a fish with a hook in its mouth diving to get away from the fisherman.

Slocum rubbed his fingers over the rock and scraped enough to show a bright yellow streak. If this wasn't the same vein he had found higher up, he would eat it one stone at a time. Somebody had come up underneath and had worked out a considerable amount of the blue dirt.

High-graders.

He swung around and cast his light into the distance. The tunnel curved enough to swallow up the light and not show him anything. Slocum examined the wet slope up into the Low Down tunnel above and knew he could never climb back. Not only was the steady stream of water against him, making the stone too slippery to climb, it was too steep. Even if he could jump and catch the edge of the drift above, pulling up into it wasn't likely to happen.

Slocum walked a dozen paces in the direction he thought was farther into the mountainside. He kept the vein at his right side until it vanished back into the wall. Then he examined the walls for signs of recent work. He was no expert, but from the sharp, bright cuts in the rock, this drift had been chopped out of the mountain less than a week earlier.

He sat heavily and thought on the matter. If someone else mined this area, it might not mean high-grading. That their tunnel ran under the Low Down's was one thing, but they might have found another section of the vein on their own. For all he knew, Morgan Haining might not have any claim to this part of the strike.

He decided it was something a lawyer—or a lawman—would have to discover. From what he knew of Morgan Haining, he doubted the man intentionally stole another miner's gold. The Low Down operation was extensive and of some duration. All this had been cut recently and hadn't connected with the Low Down's shafts until he had blown his way downward.

Slocum got to his feet and traced back to where he had blasted through. The way the water flowed, the hole was about to be clogged with mud and rock. Where the water drilled a new channel he couldn't determine, but the floor in the tunnel where he stood was drying out fast. He continued along the tunnel, going toward what had to be the mouth. Before he had walked a dozen paces, he felt a gentle breeze blowing against his face and wet clothing, chilling him. He sped up, then stopped suddenly when he came to an intersecting tunnel.

Soft rustling sounds came from the right branch of the tunnel. Ahead, he knew, lay open air. The breeze was stronger now than before, but the sounds drew him like a magnet draws iron filings. He wanted to find out what was going on with this spiderweb of tunnels that ran in directions no sane miner would dig.

Slocum knew that might be the problem. Seldom had he found a prospector who wasn't as crazy as a bedbug. The years of isolation turned them loco, and if they had partners, both men were likely to be insane. But digging at odd angles, some parallel to what must be the face of the mountain, went beyond crazy. Miners worked like beavers to burrow into the hard rock, but they did so with the determination of finding gold. Wasting so much time and sweat digging the crossing tunnels made no sense.

The sounds faded to utter silence. Slocum had long since regained his hearing after the powerful explosion that had brought him here, but he knew he might miss some faint sound. He reached up and turned down his carbide light until he got only a flickering glow. Then he covered it with his hand and plunged into utter darkness. Waiting for his eyes to adjust, he finally saw a distant reflection of a miner's candle against the rock wall, moving down the tunnel. Spots of quartz caught and twisted the flickering light but gave him enough illumination to advance one step at a time.

He might be walking into a rattler's den, but he had to find out. Someone had tried to kill him in the Low Down. And others were digging tunnels along the vein of gold that Haining needed in order to keep the Low Down operational. Slocum wanted to find out who was behind it all.

His slow pace allowed whoever carried the candle to get ahead. He came to another junction. The mountain had to be a honeycomb of tunnels, all running at strange angles. A drift would meander along following a vein of ore, but this curious arrangement had no rhyme or reason Slocum could determine.

And he wasn't able to tell where the person he followed had gone, either. Dropping to the ground, he pressed his ear down hard. At first all he heard was the slow dripping of water from his clothes, but then came a shuffling sound. He found which of the tunnels the noise came from and advanced cautiously, occasionally letting out a little light to show him the way. The candle had disappeared entirely.

Then came a noise he couldn't figure out.

"A woman crying," he said aloud.

"Who's there? Show yourself!" a frightened voice answered his declaration.

"Is that you, Evie?"

"John?"

He took his hand away from in front of the carbide lamp and turned up the intensity. The carbide sizzled and hissed as more of the mineral dissolved in the water. Silhouetted in yet another juncture ahead stood Evangeline Haining, wiping away tears and looking distraught while trying not to show it.

"I'm so glad you found me, John. B-but what are you doing here?"

She was on the verge of blubbering. The dark-haired woman wiped away more tears and took a deep breath to compose herself. Slocum kept his distance, unsure what was causing her to be so distraught.

"Why are you crying?"

"I . . . I'm lost and my candle burned out. I know it was stupid, and I should have taken a few spares. I know they don't burn for all that long, but I forgot to bring matches and—" She dashed to him and threw her arms around his neck. Her strong grip almost crushed the air from his lungs. She sobbed heavily as she clung to him. Slocum gingerly put his arms around her until the worst of the emotions had faded.

She looked up. Her blue eyes gleamed in the light from his carbide lamp.

"You're wet? How'd you get wet in a mine?"

"I lost my canoe," he said. Evangeline frowned but Slocum wasn't inclined to go into details. "What do you mean you're lost? The juncture where I first heard you was the way out. All you had to do was turn to your left and you would have been outside." He didn't bother adding, "Wherever outside is."

"I . . . I didn't know. I came into the mine and got lost. There are so many tunnels going this way and that. I got turned around and confused."

"Then your candle burned out."

"That's when you found me. Let's get out of here, John. I'm so scared. I should never have gone in like that."

Slocum knew she was impetuous and that it had gotten her into trouble. If he hadn't found her, she might have wandered the endless maze of tunnels until she died of thirst or fell into some unseen pit. He noted how few supporting timbers were in these drifts. Whoever had cut through the rock had done it fast and furious, not bothering with anything like safety.

"Why'd you come in at all?"

"This—these—belong to the high-graders." She motioned all around her. "I followed a trail to the other side of the mountain, almost opposite the Low Down, and saw a single entrance. No tailings to speak of, but evidence that rock had been moved away recently."

"That's mighty suspicious," Slocum admitted. Miners seldom got rid of tailings. Better to simply dump it down the side of the mountain than waste time and effort hauling away the dross. But the high-graders were hardly the sort to worry about being found. The rough way they had cut these tunnels showed that. They were intent on getting in, following the Low Down's mother lode, and chipping off as much as they could. Slocum had no doubt they would have disappeared like morals in a cathouse if they'd ever been found out.

"How'd you know where to look?" Slocum had the uneasy feeling Evangeline had been set up. Someone had intended her to find these tunnels and get lost in them.

"I overheard two men talking. I couldn't identify them. I . . . I was eavesdropping from behind a wall, the one over by my house. They were walking along the path and I was gardening, down on my hands and knees where they couldn't see me. Or I them. I know it wasn't polite to spy, but there was no way not to overhear what they said. One whispered that they were getting ready to suck all the gold out of the Low Down like a, well, what he said was crude. The meaning was clear, though. They had found the big vein of ore and were intending on stealing it."

Slocum considered what Evangeline had said. He doubted the men had intentionally spoken to lure her into the mine.

"They gave directions here and you just came to check it out?"

"More or less. Well, I figured from a few clues where to find the opening. It took me the better part of the afternoon riding around in my buggy, but I located this mine from their description, and you know the rest."

Slocum put his arm around her and guided the woman toward the juncture leading out. Or was it? He took a few minutes to study the footprints on the floor to determine the way back. It helped that his boots were wet and had left distinct footprints in the dust.

"I should have soaked my shoes in water, too," Evangeline said, joking. "This is better than marking the way with chalk."

"But you didn't bring chalk, did you?"

"Why, no. I had no idea what I'd find. The candle was on a shelf near the mouth of the mine. That's where the miners always keep them." She caught her breath and then said, "Sorry, John. I forgot that you're a miner. You know those things."

"Not that well," Slocum said. "I'm more at home branding cattle or breaking horses."

"How wonderful you ended up working for Papa," she said, holding his arm and resting her cheek against it. "I'm lucky to have found you."

"You've got it backwards," Slocum said. "I found you." Before she could reply, he put a grimy hand over her mouth and turned the carbide lamp toward the wall to block most of its light.

"Someone's ahead!" Evangeline couldn't keep quiet. She had heard what he already had. That told him his hearing had returned to normal.

"Quiet," he said. Slocum wondered if they ought to retreat or hold their ground. He decided to do neither. "Stay behind me but keep close."

He felt her shaking hand grip his shoulder. Slocum kept the lamp turned down to prevent it from betraying his position too early while allowing it to clearly show where he was stepping. In a few minutes they reached the juncture where he had felt the air from outside against his face.

"That's the way out," he said, pointing Evangeline in the right direction. "I want to see who's poking around in the mine down around the ore vein I found."

"I'm not leaving!" she protested. "I came here to find out who's stealing from Papa, and I won't quit now."

"They're probably armed," Slocum said.

"Don't be silly. Who wears a six-shooter into a mine?

Why, what do those things weigh? Three pounds? Four? That's too much iron to lug around for no reason. More likely, they'd have knives or pickaxes."

"Either can slit your throat or bash in your head," he told her.

"Then we'll have to sneak up on them so they don't hear."

Slocum considered dragging Evangeline out of the mine for her own good. But that would alert the high-graders, and he didn't want to get into a fight with them in a tunnel. In spite of her logic, the high-graders might be armed, especially if they weren't working as miners. He had seen enough men drifting around Cripple Creek who wore their hoglegs low on their hips and had the look of gunfighters about them. It wasn't much of a jump from gunfighter to outlaw willing to steal another man's gold.

In spite of all that, he had to agree with the woman. His curiosity was such that he wanted to find out the identities of the high-graders, too. It made more sense to leave the mine, find a hidden spot, and wait for the owlhoots to leave. After learning who they were, he could determine what the best way of dealing with them might be.

That was what logic told him to do. Instead, he said to Evangeline, "Don't say a word and keep behind me. At the first sign of trouble, run like hell."

"Go on, John, go on. Hurry. We don't want to lose them."

"We won't. I know exactly where they're heading."

He turned down the carbide lamp to its lowest intensity. The flame sputtered and hissed, always on the verge of going out. Slocum thought about turning it off entirely, but after his tumultuous slide into this mine and the fear of dying in the dark, he kept it on.

Voices ahead warned him when they were close.

". . . got enough here to make us rich," one voice said. The tunnel distorted the voice and prevented Slocum from identifying the speaker.

"We should think on gettin' a bigger cut," said another man. "We're bein' cheated, you know."

"You shut yer mouth. We ain't double-crossin' *him*. If he got wind of it, he'd cut yer damn tongue from yer mouth."

"You afraid of him?"

"Damned right I am!"

"We could be rich. Look at that there vein and tell me if it ain't the purtiest thing you ever did see."

"There was a whore in San Antonio once—"

"Shut up," snapped the second man. "You know what I mean. You can buy every damn whore in Colorado with the kind of money that gold'd get us."

Silence fell. Slocum edged forward, turning the lamp around and pointing it toward the juncture that would take him and Evangeline to the outer world. He wanted to get just a glimpse of the men. Slocum knew that would be all it'd take for him to either identify them outright or be able to later.

He just wished the rugged mine walls and the way the tunnels moseyed around didn't distort their voices so.

"Let me see, John."

"Hush," he said, pushing Evangeline back behind him. He didn't think she had spoken loudly enough to be overheard, but the men in the tunnel weren't saying a word. Slocum conjured up images of an ambush. Guns trained on the tunnel. The instant he poked his head around, lead would fly. He knew it was a possibility, but he had to see.

Arm out to hold Evangeline behind him, he inched forward until he came to the bend in the tunnel. The way he remembered it, the exposed vein of gold-bearing ore stretched along the wall here. He chanced a quick peek around and drew back in the same motion.

"Well? Who's there, John?"

"Quiet," he said. "I didn't see anyone." He thought hard. This had been a dead end. Or he had thought it was. He had been too intent on getting out of the mine with the news of the high-graders to properly explore. But that didn't mean the two outlaws weren't waiting to blow his head off if he walked into plain view.

"You hear more than the pair of them?"

"No, but—"

Slocum gave the knurled knob on the carbide lamp a savage twist and swung it around, aiming it like he would a six-shooter. If he blinded them for an instant, he could take them both.

His light bathed the quartz and the gleaming flecks of gold inside. And nothing else. The high-graders were nowhere to be seen.

9

"Where did they go?" Evangeline stepped past Slocum and looked around, using her hand to shield her eyes from the glare of his miner's lamp.

"There," Slocum said, stepping forward quickly. He knew they should turn tail and run, but he had gone too far already. He might be walking into a leveled six-gun, but he had to be sure. Better to get a bullet in the gut than take one in the back. Pressing against the rocky wall, he found the fissure. It was hardly wide enough to squeeze through, but the two high-graders had done just that. Slocum saw how the natural crack bent away and vanished within a few feet. He could follow, but what was the point?

"Let's go after them, John," the woman said. "I need to know their identities so I can tell—"

"Never mind," he said, catching her around the waist and preventing her from slipping into the crevice. "They're long gone by now. But there's a way we might find who they are."

"We can go after—"

"No," he said, bodily lifting her from the floor and turning her around. "We go out the way you came in and see if we can spot anyone on the mountainside. There's got to be more than one way into this maze."

"I suppose."

"It's too dangerous going after them." Slocum told her, although he had thought to do just that. And he would have, had he been alone. "We get outside and use our eyes and our heads."

"Very well," Evangeline said dubiously. She allowed him to steer her through the tunnels and soon they were out in fresh air. Slocum sucked in the pure, clean mountain air and coughed only a bit. The crusher down the valley was working today and the mill was grinding, and the smelter would be fired up before long, sending huge plumes of black smoke into the air. But not now. He appreciated the air after being almost buried alive inside the mountain.

"There's where I came up the trail," Evangeline said. He saw a horse and buggy down below on a wide road. This was the main road to the mill.

"That might be how they got rid of the tailings," Slocum said, looking around. "All they had to do was pull up a wagon underneath and shovel it into the bed."

"Why? Why would they want rock that had been discarded?"

Slocum had no answer for that, but knowing how the high-graders had gotten rid of the tailings was a step toward figuring out what they were up to, other than pulling the rich ore out from under Morgan Haining's nose.

"Where are they, John? I don't see hide nor hair of anyone else up here." Evangeline stood on a rock and looked around like a prairie dog on sentry duty. He grabbed her around the waist and lifted her easily again, depositing her feet firmly on the ground beside him.

"Don't let them catch a glimpse of you. They'd know we were on to their scheme."

"Whatever that scheme is," she said glumly.

"We know part of it. That vein of ore near the fissure belongs to the Low Down Mine. They're mining gold that rightfully belongs to your pa."

"That's good enough to get the law down here, isn't it?

We can chase them off and—what's wrong, John? You look angry."

"Chasing them away isn't enough for me. I want them brought to justice." His fingers rubbed up and down across the spot on his left hip where his cross-draw holster usually rested. "They tried to kill me. Might be they already killed Thompson and Bowden."

"But that was an accident. Mines are dangerous."

"They are," Slocum said, but he didn't bother telling her how he had found the sawed-through timber that had almost spelled his end. He would have been drowned if he hadn't blasted his way free.

"What aren't you telling me?" Evangeline looked at him with her clear blue eyes and a vision into his soul that he didn't much cotton to right now.

"Let's go on down to the road and make our way back. Might be your pa can be convinced to do something about this." He pointed uphill to the mouth of the hidden mine where the high-graders had worked so diligently to steal the richest vein of ore discovered in Cripple Creek in more than a year.

"What of those men who got away?"

"If they spot us, it'll look like I'm just taking you out for a late afternoon ride. If we see them first, we'll have to decide what to do then." Slocum's mind raced ahead. He could always unhitch Evangeline's horse from her buggy and ride bareback to chase down the high-graders. But he had to find the pair first.

He didn't. As much as both he and Evangeline hunted, they saw nobody astride a horse. Everyone they passed drove the heavily laden ore wagons to the mill or empty ones returning from delivering their rocky cargoes.

Slocum drove directly back to the Low Down office set atop the hill overlooking the mouth of the mine. He saw that a saddled horse was tethered behind the building.

"That's Papa's favorite horse," Evangeline said. "I'm glad he's in the office. Let's speak to him about this terrible matter right now."

Slocum was less inclined to go in. He looked like he had been pulled through a knothole backwards, and he didn't want Evangeline spilling too much too soon. He wondered about Haining employing a man like Lucas Miles, but that might have been nothing more than necessity, knowledgeable foremen being hard to find. Miles hadn't shown a whole lot of experience, even to a greenhorn miner like Slocum.

"Papa, Papa!" Evangeline opened the door and blew in like a summer storm. "I must speak to you immediately. *We* must," she amended when Slocum trailed her into the office.

Morgan Haining looked up. His face was drawn and he looked paler than when Slocum had met him for the first time, but the smile he gave his daughter was genuine.

"Evie, to what do I owe this fine visit? You know I'm working."

"I—we—have information about men stealing from the Low Down," she said. She sat in the chair opposite Haining's desk and almost dared him to contradict her, but Slocum saw the words forming on the man's lips before she had finished her accusation.

"You and Slocum?" He looked at Slocum and frowned. "Why aren't you at work? The shift's not over for another hour."

"We found evidence of high-graders," Evangeline said, as if her father's question meant nothing. But to Slocum it did. He had to explain.

"Miles ordered me to blast down a new drift. The timbers collapsed and I was trapped."

"Obviously not trapped," Haining said. "You are standing here in front of me."

"Papa—"

"I used the nitro to blow out the floor. I ended up in a tunnel cut under yours in the Low Down."

"I don't understand a bit of this. You used nitroglycerin? Why? It's far too expensive, and I have given orders not to use it."

"It's mighty dangerous because it's so unstable," Slocum

said. "Miles ordered it. And then the roof collapsed. But the tunnels I found were—"

"I'll speak to Mr. Miles about this right away. Why, that's a waste of precious money. Even with the new vein you unearthed, there's little enough to go around after I pay for . . ." Haining trailed off, then fixed his gaze on Slocum as if he had almost revealed some deep, dark secret.

"High-graders, Papa. I was in their tunnels, too. They are digging out ore that rightfully belongs to the Low Down."

"I don't think so," Haining said. "That's not possible."

"Who owns the side of the mountain opposite to the Low Down?" Slocum asked.

"I do. I own the entire mountain. There used to be a trio of cranky old coots who worked that side of the hill, but they weren't miners as much as prospectors. They had no desire to prove their claim. I bought them out—at a fair price, I should say. I don't know where they went. Utah, I think."

"Who's been working that claim?"

"Why, no one. The mines were all shuttered."

"They looked mighty wide open to me," Slocum said.

"Mr. Miles tended to that. He would not have disobeyed me."

"Ask him, Papa."

Slocum heard a hardness come to the woman's voice. He remembered how she and Miles had had a little run-in, and how the foreman had come out second best. Evangeline had no love for the man, that much was certain.

"There's no need. He reported to me that it was done. I remember distinctly."

"He—" began Evangeline, but her father held up his hand and cut her off.

"Don't argue. And this business about high-graders is absurd. What problems we've had were those felt by other mines, also."

"I can show you where they're digging out your ore,"

Slocum said. "The vein takes a downward turn from the Low Down and they burrowed in underneath."

"Slocum, I can chastise my daughter. I can fire you for insubordination. Miles has said there is no trouble in the mine, from men stealing the gold, or from any exterior situation. What disruption there is in the flow of gold has been caused by internal problems."

"Reckon that's so," Slocum said, knowing his idea of "internal problems" was entirely different from Haining's.

"I'm glad you say so," Haining said caustically. "Now if you will leave, I've got work to do." He looked up at Slocum. "And you do, also. I am not sure I appreciate you loafing on the job and being with my daughter."

Slocum said nothing. He left while Evangeline argued with her father a few minutes longer. The woman came from the office looking disconsolate.

"He won't listen. He just won't."

"Does Miles have that kind of hold over him? All he needed to do was come look at the high-graders' work. I believe him when he says he owns the entire mountain. That means they *are* stealing his gold."

"The richest find," Evangeline said glumly.

"You might sweet-talk him into getting into the mines to see," Slocum suggested.

Evangeline shook her head. The wind caught her dark hair and sent it out around her face like a gossamer frame. Although she was almost as filthy from poking around in the mine as Slocum, he thought she had never looked prettier.

"Mama has been talking to him. She's always nagging him about something, and this is his way of keeping her from making too much of a fuss over the way he spends so much of the money."

Slocum considered the situation. A wife wanting a bigger share of what her husband earned was not unusual, but Slocum heard something more in what Evangeline said that he didn't understand.

"What's he spend so much on? He agonizes over it from the way he talks of all his accounts."

Evangeline hesitated, then said, "I shouldn't tell you since Papa keeps this quiet. He's not one to brag, but he supports many of the injured miners."

"How's that?" Slocum wasn't sure what she meant. "He hired Randolph and his son, and I doubt they'd have found jobs anywhere else, being deaf as posts, but that's hardly supporting a man who isn't pulling his weight." Slocum knew the two men worked harder than any three other miners, and that included putting himself into the equation.

"That's only part of it, and that doesn't cost him money. Oh, as salary, but he gets a good day's work from both of them. No, he *supports* miners injured in the mines. One man had a leg cut off. Another is blind. Others have a variety of injuries, but most have difficulty breathing."

Slocum coughed and knew how easily his lungs had filled with grit from the mine. Being trapped in a space hardly larger than a coffin filled with dust took away a man's wind mighty fast.

"He pays for them to live?" Slocum had never heard of such a thing. Most mine owners fired any injured miner.

"He says it's only right. If a man is injured through no fault of his own, the mine owner—Papa—must do what he can to help them get by."

"How many miners is he keeping alive like this?"

"Several. Well, ten or so. They have another bunkhouse at the far side of Cripple Creek, and Papa makes sure they eat regular meals and have what medical care is possible in a mining town like this."

"I don't think this notion will catch on with the other mine owners."

"No, I am sure it won't, but Papa had help growing up and wants to do what he can to smooth out the potholes in the road of life for others."

"So your ma doesn't think much of his charity?"

"She had a more favored upbringing," Evangeline said. Slocum saw the conflict spread out where he could examine it more carefully. Darleen Haining saw no reason for her husband to spend one red cent on anyone but her, while his guilt caused him to want to do what he could for men injured on the job in his mine. She slackened off on the criticism if he ignored the threat posed by the high-graders.

The only way Darleen Haining came out ahead that way was if she shared in the gold stolen by the owlhoots. She let him give a few dollars to the crippled miners while she raked off even more illegally.

"Tell me about your ma," Slocum said. "I didn't get much of a look at her before. Is she the kind of woman who'd cheat on your pa?"

"I—" Evangeline clamped her mouth shut. "I cannot say," she said in a neutral tone.

Slocum let the matter drop. He had an idea what was going on, but getting Haining to believe it might be a real chore.

"So? Can you convince him to take a look at the tunnels on the other side of the mountain?"

"I doubt it," she said. "He does not like to be confined. He becomes very nervous in a small room. I cannot imagine what Papa would do if he went into a mine, with its low roofs and narrow passageways."

"Seems he went into the wrong business," Slocum said. "There's not much he can do to personally check to see if anyone's stealing from him if he can't abide by a tight tunnel or overhanging rock."

"What you say is true, John. I don't know where to go with this." She looked up at him and said in a voice so low he almost didn't catch what she was saying, "I want to thank you for all you've done."

"Getting your pa to get the law involved—or even other mine owners—will be thanks enough. I don't like seeing any man robbed, even if he is doing as much as possible to let it happen."

"That wasn't what I meant, John. And I think you know it." Evangeline stepped closer and looked up at him. Her blue eyes were bright and hot with desire. "Being so close to death did something to me. It excited me. I don't know why, but it did. Or might be just being so close to you is what excites me." She reached out and slid her fingers down his belly between his waistband and his shirt. Those fingers burrowed lower and caused him to look around uncomfortably.

"I don't think your pa would appreciate seeing you doing that, not after he made it mighty clear I ought to give you a wide berth."

"He doesn't own me. And you're doing more to save him from himself than anyone else. I appreciate that. I appreciate you," Evangeline said, digging down even more in his pants. Her fingers found his slowly stiffening organ. "And I appreciate *this*." Her fingers curled around him and tried to squeeze, but the angle was too extreme for her to grip without hurting her wrist.

"Not here," he said.

"I know the place," she said. "There's a secluded pool not far from our house. Hot water bubbles up in the pond."

"It probably smells like sulphur," Slocum said.

"I'll make sure you won't ever notice a little thing like that," Evangeline promised, grinning broadly. The expression on her face told him she would do just that.

"Go on. I'll follow."

"Don't be long," the dark-haired beauty said. She gave him a quick little stroke before pulling her hand from his pants. "Don't be long *getting* to me," she amended. "Once you find me, remember that there's something else that I *do* like long." Laughing, she hurried off.

Slocum watched the young woman as she left, marvelling at how she could seem so prim one minute and downright wanton the next. When she looked back over her shoulder, he knew there was nothing prim and proper about what she intended.

He looked back at the closed door of the mining company office and wondered what Morgan Haining would do if he got wind of what was about to happen to his daughter—with her full consent. Then Slocum shrugged it off. Evangeline was old enough to know her own mind. She certainly had a better idea of how to run a gold mine than her father. And possibly far better than what her mother would do.

Rather than take the path and follow Evangeline, he cut across the rugged countryside, going over the side of a steep hill and finally reaching the base, where he circled. The sulphur smell was stronger here. He knew rich folks paid huge amounts of money to take the waters on the far side of the Rockies. At Manitou Springs the Navajo water was supposed to cure all ills. As Slocum walked along, there was only one ill he wanted cured. It grew increasingly painful to walk as he thought about Evangeline Haining naked in the pool of water, waiting for him.

Although he had already been expecting the sight of her to be just about the best part of their encounter, the mirage that appeared caused his erection to try to do a cartwheel in his pants. Evangeline was stark naked and draped like some mermaid across a large, smooth rock beside the pool. She lay back, arms stretched over her head and her long legs dangling down so that her toes were barely rippling the water in the pool.

He hardly knew what to look at. Her firm breasts were flattened by the way her back arched, and she flowed over the rock like a sunbathing feline. The long legs, moving slowly and causing ripples in the pond, were enticing. But Slocum's eyes moved up those slender legs to the dark, crinkly furred nest between her thighs. Dewdrops caught the afternoon sun and glistened there. He wasn't sure if that moisture came from the pond or from the woman's arousal.

Slocum intended to find out.

He was removing his clothing as he approached the pond. He started to call out to her and then had a better idea. Discarding shirt and boots, he sat on the side of the pool. His nostrils flared at the heavy sulphur bubbling up from the depths of the Earth. It was hard for him to think of this volcanically heated pool and then remember how cold and dank it was down in the Low Down's deepest levels. He rocked back and skinned out of his pants. He let out a small sigh of relief when he freed his erection from the cloth prison.

Without making even a small splash, he slid into the warm water and dog-paddled to a spot just under where Evangeline lolled. She hadn't noticed him yet. He stopped swimming and found a spot where he could stand on the bottom of the shallow pool without losing his balance. With a sudden grab, both of his strong hands circled her slender ankle and tugged. She slid down the slick rock and didn't even get a chance to cry out before she hit the water.

By then, Slocum was already swarming around her, swimming under her flailing arms and coming up behind her. His hardness spread her warm buttocks as he reached around her, one hand resting on her belly and the other clamping down firmly over her breasts. He felt her frenzied heartbeat and knew she was ready for him.

"Oh!" Evangeline gasped when his hand moved lower than her belly and found the tangled mat of her bush. His finger curled about and slipped into her heated channel. "That had better be you, John Slocum."

"Were you expecting anyone else?" he whispered in her ear. Then he nibbled just a bit on the dangling lobe. This caused Evangeline to go limp. She floated in the water, her legs coming to the surface as she lay back atop him.

He moved his way up beneath her, letting his natural buoyancy lift him. Her legs parted and he came up between them. She reached down and gripped his steely length.

"What have I found in the water?"

"Something that doesn't want to stay in the water. It wants to get into you," Slocum said. His hands moved down and parted her legs even more, but reaching around her prevented him from stroking over her belly and lower.

"Like this?" Evangeline bucked a little, then resettled down in the water. As she came down, he slid easily into her lubricated interior. The water had been warm; where he was now buried was burning hot. When she tensed and clamped her strong inner muscles down, he gasped and thrashed about beneath her.

They rolled over in the water, both facedown, but stayed this way for only a few seconds before rolling onto their backs again. Evangeline locked her legs around his to keep him firmly within her. He began stroking his hands up and down her chest, finding the twin mounds of her breasts, teasing and toying with them, then moving on to slip his hands over her sides and down to her legs. Her rear end fit perfectly into the curve of his groin, but there was no way he could stroke.

The pressures she exerted on his buried manhood sent sharp jolts of pleasure into his loins. He tried arching up but only succeeded in dunking himself. Evangeline seemed to understand how they lacked leverage.

"It's so nice just resting within me, but I want more, too, John," she said. Her hands moved around and cupped his muscular ass, and then they rolled over and over in the water before coming up against the bouldered shoreline of the pond. Somehow, she managed to get halfway out of the water and pressed herself facedown on the rock. Her arms stretched high over her head, duplicating the position he had seen her in when he had approached the pond.

The difference this time was that she pressed her chest down into the rock—and he was hidden balls-deep within her from behind.

He got his feet under him and found a spot that gave him leverage. He slid forward, burying himself entirely in her tightness. Pulling back, he paused a moment. The warm water lapping around his balls provided little relief for what he wanted. He slid easily back into her tightness. Her muscles again massaged him, gripped him, tried to milk him of his fiery seed.

Slocum began stroking with long, powerful thrusts that lifted the woman out of the water every time he sank into her. She sagged when he withdrew, begging for him to return. He did. He had to. His body was rushing ahead of his wish to make this last as long as possible. Desire crashed over Evangeline, and she cried out while her body shook as if she had contracted some ague. But the emotional release was not yet hers, even if the physical was.

"More, John, don't stop. Oh, damn you, don't stop. Give me every inch, every damned inch!"

He began pistoning forward harder and faster. This robbed Evangeline of her coherent speech. Only trapped-animal sounds escaped her lips. He stroked over her sides and then gripped her hips to pull them back into the circle of his groin as he rammed forward. He felt as if he were on fire, burning from the tip of his shaft all the way down deep into his body. That heat spread like a prairie wildfire through his belly and chest and finally exploded in his head as he spilled his seed into her yearning cavity.

Evangeline cried out again with ultimate ecstasy, but Slocum was locked in physical release of his own. When he began to melt within her heated core, he stepped away, lost his balance, and splashed noisily in the pool.

The woman turned and grinned at him. She reached up, cupped her own breasts, and tweaked the nipples. Then she slid her fingers down in a *V* toward her crotch.

"You got anything left? I need it."

"Insatiable bitch," he growled as he paddled around in the sulphur water pool.

"That's me," Evangeline said, laughing. Then she slid beneath the water, and the next thing Slocum knew she was poking her head up between his legs. Her eager lips took his limp length and worked it back to a usable stiffness. It was after sunset before they left the pool and lounged on the rapidly cooling rocks.

"I'd better get home. I don't want Papa worrying about me."

"He should have," Slocum said, watching as she climbed into her discarded clothes. The sight of her bare, damp flesh vanishing behind her clothing was almost as exciting as watching her undress. He let out a sigh and knew he had to get back to the bunkhouse himself. The miners would be wondering what had happened to him.

Lucas Miles might well have told them that he had died

when the mine shaft collapsed. If he had, Slocum wanted to see the foreman's face when he found that it wasn't true.

But leaving Evangeline was still difficult, no matter how much he wanted to get Miles's goat.

10

"What the hell happened, Slocum?" Lucas Miles glared at him with a combination of anger and disbelief.

"What do you mean?" Slocum decided to play it cagy and see if Miles would come right out and say that he had sawed through the timbers and tried to bury him alive. Slocum wished he had been able to talk with Billy, but the young miner had been sent on a trip into Cripple Creek to pick up supplies, since the usual freighter had up and disappeared.

"You were supposed to blast in the lower drift yesterday. What happened?"

"I blasted but hit water. It took some doing to get out, but I did. I reckon you'll have to dig through the spot where the timbers gave way, because of the water."

"Water? We got water in the mine?" Half a dozen miners crowded around to hear Slocum's report. "The pump's not workin' worth beans," another said. The chorus of fear and apprehension that spread through the group that was assembled and ready to go down into the mines drowned out Miles's protests.

"There ain't no danger!" the foreman finally roared. "Slocum don't know what he's talkin' about."

"Doesn't take much for a man to know if there's water in the mine," said a nearby miner. "How about it, Slocum?"

"There's water on the lower level. When I blasted through the end of the drift, it began draining into yet another tunnel. Don't rightly know where it came from since it was under ours."

"The whole danged mountain's full of tunnels. Been years since the first prospector came," Miles said. "The water's filled up this other tunnel? The one you claim's below the Low Down?"

"I'm saying it is," Slocum said. "Go look."

"No need," Miles said hastily. "The ore vein wouldn't go in that direction. We'll follow it from the next level up."

"Pump not work so good," Randolph said. "I check. It not work."

"You won't need the damn pump," flared Miles. "The mine is safe. There's no flooding."

"There won't be on higher levels," Slocum said. "Only on the one where you wanted me to blast with the nitro."

"Nitro? So much explosive?" Randolph shook his head.

"Herk, Singer, get your asses down into the mine and check it for water. Now!"

Miles's two henchmen looked uneasy at the thought of going to the bottom of the mine, but both jumped onto the elevator and signaled for the operator to lower away.

"The rest of you malingerers," Miles said, "get yourselves over and load wagons with ore. I won't have you actin' like royalty while others have to work."

Slocum wanted to inspect the mine and see the extent of the sawed mine supports, but he joined Randolph and his son taking ore from the huge piles and dumping it into a wagon. With so many men working, it took only a short while for the wagon to be groaning under the weight of the rock on its way down the valley to the mill.

"Nuthin' wrong, boss," called Herk as he swung from the elevator and dropped to the ground.

"Then why are boots wet?" Randolph pointed.

"Oh, there's some seepage, but nuthin' to worry over," Herk said hastily. "You might wanna shutter that level 'til you got a chance to check it personally."

"There's no floodin'?" Miles asked. Slocum watched the foreman carefully. The man was upset over the notion that an underground river had been tapped. Because it might flood the mine from which he undercut the Low Down's vein of gold and ruin his schemes for high-grading? Slocum would have bet all his pay and twice his bonus on that one and wouldn't have lost.

How could he convince Haining that his foreman was robbing him blind?

Miles went and talked several minutes with his two cronies. Slocum took the time to go over and greet Billy, who was just pulling up in the company's second wagon.

"Get to unloadin' that, you two," called Miles. The foreman turned back to his intense discussion with Herk and Singer.

"What happened to you, Slocum?" Billy hopped to the ground and slapped Slocum on the back. "You're a sight for sore eyes. I thought you was dead or worse."

"What's worse?"

"Still down in that mine, alive and scratchin' at rock to get free."

"That's worse," Slocum agreed. "Why didn't you come down to help drill the holes and blast?"

"Him," Billy said, jerking his thumb in Miles's direction. "He tole me Randolph or somebody else was helpin' you. He put me to drivin' this damn wagon. Don't get near as much money bein' a freighter as I do underground." He looked up into the sky mottled with gray storm clouds. "Don't much like the weather. Bein' up here you can get rained on."

Slocum had to laugh, then sobered when he realized how things locked together perfectly. Miles had told him to use the heavier explosive to make it seem that Slocum had either accidentally or carelessly blown himself up. No one would have looked at the mine's support timbers, and the entire drift would have been closed off, giving him a grave without a tombstone. As it was, the water might have saved

Slocum's life. Waiting for rescue that would never have come could have exhausted his air. He might not have known he was even dying as the air got worse and worse. But the rising water had forced him to risk using the nitro in the enclosed space.

"You two, get on down into the mine," barked Miles.

"I can get back to real work? Hooray!" Billy threw his dusty hat high in the air and then caught it when it drifted back down.

"I got to get on up to talk with Mr. Haining," Miles said. He spun and stalked off, leaving Slocum to wonder why the foreman had bothered to mention that. It wasn't any concern to a miner.

"Where'd Herk and Singer get off to?" Slocum asked.

"Who the hell cares? They're all the time goldbricking while the rest of us are down there minin' the gold. Ain't fair, but what is in this life? You ready, Slocum?"

"What're we doing today?" Slocum asked. He swung onto the elevator platform. Randolph and his son Ira joined them.

"Don't know. Lemme ask." Billy turned and called to the elevator operator, "Jonesy, what're—"

"What's wrong?" Slocum asked when Billy cut off his question so abruptly.

"That's not Jonesy workin' the elevator."

"So?" The word had barely left Slocum's lips when the platform twisted like a thing come alive under them. He grabbed for the railing. It came loose, tumbling down twenty stories to the bottom of the shaft. Slocum scrambled to get his feet under him. Then the platform bucked like a bronco and sent him flying.

He let out a cry of surprise and grabbed frantically at a rope dangling down. He caught it, felt it burning the palms of his hands for a few feet, and then he jerked to a halt beneath the tilted elevator. Looking up, he saw how the two Randolphs were fighting to remain on top of the platform, now tilted at a forty-five-degree angle. Billy was moaning and lying on the platform, his head lower than his feet.

"Billy!"

"Can't help ya, Slocum, my feet're all tangled up." Billy tried to sit up, but the slope was too great and from the way he moaned, he was hurt.

"Ira!" Slocum saw the younger Randolph coming to life. "Get the elevator level." Slocum fought to hang on. For some reason, his left arm was weakening fast. He had no time to see why. He was too intent on not falling to his death. There was no way he could hope to survive a two-hundred-foot fall.

Ira Randolph saw the trouble, made sure his pa was safe, then checked Billy. Then he slid to the edge of the platform, dangling half off, and reached down for Slocum to take his hand. The elevator platform gave another abrupt lurch that almost sent Ira to his death. The young man held on grimly.

Billy was roaring for the elevator operator to do something. But the winch was smoking, and inch by inch the rope was burning away from the friction of the slippage.

Ira made another grab for Slocum just as his hands weakened so much he could no longer hold onto the rope. Slocum fell a few inches and then snapped around, Ira's powerful hand circling his right wrist.

"Swing me back and forth," Slocum called. "Do it. Do it and I'll tell you when to let me go."

Ira Randolph shook his head furiously. He had no intention of letting go. From the way his fingers slipped around Slocum's wrist, though, it wouldn't be long before the best intention meant nothing. Both men were sweating profusely, and it made the grip increasingly slippery.

Kicking his feet, Slocum began to swing like a pendulum. He saw how Ira's sleeve stretched to the breaking point as his muscles expanded in an effort to keep Slocum from falling. At the far end of his swing, Slocum yelled, "Let me go. Now!"

Whether Ira heard and obeyed or simply ran out of steam, Slocum didn't know. He fell a sickening few feet, then was scrambling furiously to get into the first level. His boots touched solid rock, and he threw himself forward as hard as he could. Landing on his belly, he lay gasping for breath. It took several seconds for him to realize he was safe. More than safe. No part of him remained in the elevator shaft.

He got his feet under him and lurched back.

"Can you jump off?" he called to Ira. "I'm safe on the first level."

Ira had gone back to his pa. The larger, older Randolph freed himself and slid, then flung himself outward. His launch wasn't as good as Slocum's, and he missed the edge of the level. Slocum made a wild grab and got a double handful of the miner's shirt. His left arm went numb from the fingers all the way to his shoulder, but his right clung to the falling man. Randolph slammed hard into the side of the shaft.

Slocum lay on his belly, holding Randolph's shirt with only his right hand. The miner got his fingers over the edge of the rocky verge and began pulling himself upward. Slocum tugged until he saw red. His vision was collapsing into a narrow tunnel, and even this was going away, leaving him blind. Then the weight on his right arm suddenly vanished.

"Randolph!"

"No worry, Slocum. You save me."

Slocum collapsed in relief, then forced himself to stand up again. There were two more men to save.

Then he saw there was only one. Ira Randolph jumped and was caught by his father, who spun him around and planted his feet safely within the mine.

"Can you get free, Billy?"

"No way," the trapped miner said. "But the platform's not creaking like it did. All the weight's off it. All but me."

"I'll get you untangled," Slocum said, gauging distances

and crouching to jump. But his legs weren't up to the task. He tried to jump but went nowhere. He thought he had finally collapsed, then felt strong hands holding him back. Both of the Randolphs had prevented him from going to Billy's rescue.

"What are you doing? I've got to—" Slocum watched in horror as the elevator platform broke free and Billy, still tangled in rope, plunged past. The falling wood platform made a whistling sound that ended seconds later with a horrendous crash. Slocum closed his eyes and tried to imagine a world where he hadn't heard Billy's death screams. He couldn't. Worse, he heard Billy pleading for Slocum to save him.

Both of the other miners pulled him away from the edge of the shaft, as if they feared he might fall after Billy.

"He is gone," Randolph said.

"Why'd you stop me? I could have gotten him free from the ropes. I—"

Slocum's eyes widened when he saw what Ira did. The young miner was holding an arm. Slocum's arm. He felt nothing. Slocum stared at the bloody mess and wondered if it had somehow been ripped from his body, then traced it back and saw the shoulder was still connected. But there wasn't any feeling in it.

"Hey, down there. Everyone all right?"

"One dead," Randolph called back. "Billy not make it."

"Damnation," came Lucas Miles's curse. Slocum had to wonder if the foreman was mad at losing a miner—or at losing the wrong one. Somehow, this had less the feel of an accident and more of another attempt to kill him.

"Droppin' a ladder. Get yer asses on up to the top," Miles shouted.

"Slocum, he cannot climb."

"I'll lower a sling for him."

"You go on up," Slocum said. "Both of you. You pull me up."

Randolph stared hard at Slocum, then solemnly nodded.

He understood. It took the better part of an hour before Slocum finally sat on a bench some distance away from the elevator. Half a dozen men worked to put a new platform in place to get the miners already in the mine out safely at the end of the shift.

"Don't know what the hell happened," Miles said, shaking his head. "Just checked them ropes a few days ago, yet they weren't up to holdin' you. Not today."

"What happened to Jonesy?" Slocum asked. He didn't know the man but Billy had. And Billy had been surprised that he wasn't working the elevator.

"Shiftless skunk," Miles said. "Got drunk last night and missed work. Don't rightly know who was runnin' the elevator. Whoever it was lit out like a scalded dog. He knew what I'd do when I caught him." Miles stared hard at Slocum and added, "He's probably in the next county by now."

"You don't know who was working the elevator?"

"That's what I said," Lucas Miles said coldly.

"Isn't that odd, the foreman not knowing who's working for him?"

"There's nuthin' that's not odd about this here mine, Slocum," Miles said. "We got miners who are damn near deaf-mutes." He glared at the Randolphs. "And we got a dead man at the bottom of the shaft because the usual elevator operator got pickled last night and couldn't work today."

Slocum winced. With surprising gentleness, Ira was cutting Slocum's sleeve away from the bloody gash that ran the length of his forearm. The fabric peeled back to reveal the open cut still oozing blood. Ira expertly bound the wound. Slocum began to wobble, woozy from the pain. But pain was better than the nothingness that had been there a few minutes earlier. He had thought he would never use his arm again.

"I lose one miner, have another all busted up."

"I can work," Slocum said. "Enough to fetch Billy from the bottom of the shaft."

"Like hell I'm lettin' you down there. You get into town and have the doc stitch you up. And this once, you have a shot or two of whiskey to ease the pain. I want you drivin' the supply wagon for a couple days 'til you heal up enough to do real work below." Miles spun about and walked away, cussing a blue streak.

"Think he'll report this to Mr. Haining?" Slocum wasn't sure who he was talking to.

Ira looked up from his bandaging chore and smiled crookedly. The young miner shook his head "no."

Slocum had to agree.

11

Slocum wrapped the reins around his right arm and gripped with his good hand. It wasn't as satisfactory as using both hands, but it controlled the tired old horses well enough to get them moving and, when necessary, stopped. From their slow pace as they trudged up the hill toward Cripple Creek, stopping them would never be a problem, only getting them to go where he wanted.

His left arm hurt like a hill of ants had taken up residence in it, but he had worried that he would lose the arm entirely. Ira Randolph had patched him up pretty well. Slocum had found afterward that the younger Randolph had a knack for doctoring, but there had never been much money in the family, so both father and son worked the mines. More than this, Ira with his hearing and speech problems wouldn't have inspired much confidence in a potential patient. Slocum had to snort in disgust at that. Most doctors he had seen inspired no confidence that they would do anything but get drunk on the money they took off their all-too-often dead patients.

Working the team, he pulled up behind the general store and jumped down after clumsily fixing the reins around the brake.

"Looks like you got bunged up somethin' fierce," the

shopkeeper said. He scratched his chin. "You workin' out at the Low Down, I reckon."

"The foreman said you had supplies ready to take back. I won't be much help loading," Slocum said, "but I'll do what I can."

"Not with that gimpy arm; you'd be more in the way than any help," the man said. "I heard about the other boy, the one who was here a couple days back. Damned shame about Billy."

"Yeah," Slocum said.

"You go on over to the Oriental or one of them other saloons, and I'll see to gettin' things loaded for you. I got to finish puttin' the flour into bags, so it'll take me a goodly hour or more."

"Sure I can't do something?"

"Nary a blessed thing, son. Git on over there. You'll have your hand full drivin' this team." The shopkeeper laughed at his small joke, pointing at Slocum's bad arm. Slocum nodded his thanks and went around to find a decent place that served a free lunch along with a beer. His belly was always complaining because the Low Down had such quick turnover in cooks. Mostly, the men taking the job did so out of desperation rather than experience. Slocum was no cook, but he knew he could do better than most of the food wranglers working at the mine.

As he climbed the steps to go into the Oriental, he paused and looked across the street at the Gentleman's Delight Drinking Emporium. He could see Herk and Singer had been in town longer than he had, because they were both roaring drunk. They jostled each other and hardly fit through the double doors, bouncing off the walls as they tried to get inside. Slocum changed his direction and followed them inside.

Miles's assistants had found themselves a table at the rear of the saloon and were already working on a full bottle of whiskey. The pile of money on the table between them made Slocum's eyes go wide. Flashing so many greenbacks like that usually meant somebody ended up unconscious—or dead—and robbed blind. Since it was the middle of the day, the saloon patrons were few and far between; besides three others, Herk, Singer, and Slocum were the only customers.

"Beer," Slocum said, situating himself so he could watch both men in the mirror behind the bar. "You got any food to go along with it?"

"For a dime I can give you a sandwich."

"It's a deal," Slocum said, dropping in front of him a nickel for the beer and a dime for the food.

The two men, for all their obvious intoxication, kept their voices low as they worked on their bottle. Slocum ate slowly, drank another beer, and was about to return to the mercantile for the supplies when both Herk and Singer shot to their feet. They grabbed the half-empty bottle and walked unsteadily from the saloon.

Slocum hunched over his beer, not looking up. They paid him no attention. But when they had finally succeeded in getting through the door, only hitting the doorjamb a couple times in their drunken hurry to get outside, he turned and followed. They had been so closemouthed that he figured they were up to something.

Both men took turns with the bottle, knocking back healthy swigs as they staggered down the street. Slocum followed them to the wheelwright's shop. His spirits sagged a mite when they went around back to where the smithy worked on his forge. Pressing himself against the side of the wheelwright's shop, Slocum peered around.

"Over there, gents," the smithy said. "You need anything else?"

"Nope, this is it," Herk said.

Slocum held his breath waiting to see what they had been so secretive about. Then he let it out when Singer and Herk hefted an axle for a freight wagon up onto their shoulders. It was heavy enough to make them stagger—or was that the effect of the booze they had been swilling? Slocum thought it must have been a little of both.

Seeing them heading in his direction, Slocum beat a hasty retreat. He watched as they made their unsteady way down the street in the direction opposite of where he had to go. Slocum was disappointed. He had expected to uncover something more nefarious than two men fetching a replacement axle for an ore wagon.

He went around to the rear of the general store. The shopkeeper sat on a rain barrel, slicing up an apple and popping the wedges into his mouth with the precision of a machine.

"You got a good sense of timin'," the merchant said. "Just this minute finished with loadin' your supplies."

"Much obliged," Slocum said. "I had lunch along with a couple beers. Almost makes it worth getting my arm all cut up."

"You got enough food loaded here for a small army. You didn't ruin your appetite now, did you?" The shopkeeper laughed, knowing the situation at the Low Down when it came to cooks.

"I'm as likely to eat the flour straight out of the sack," Slocum said. He climbed into the wagon, spent a minute wrapping the reins around his right arm, and then snapped them to get the tired draft horses pulling. They had enjoyed their respite from real work, but now they had a fully loaded wagon to contend with. They protested until Slocum found the proper pattern of snap and yell that got the pair moving.

He drove out of Cripple Creek, keeping a sharp lookout for Herk and Singer. The two men and their spare axle were nowhere to be seen. By the time he was on the main road heading back to the mine, he had given up his hunt for them. Wherever they had gone, it wasn't back to the Low Down. Slocum fell into the rattle-and-clank motion of the wagon as it bumped over rocks in the road, and almost drifted to sleep.

He came awake suddenly when he saw a masked man in the middle of the road, pointing a six-shooter at him. Slocum tried to reach for his six-shooter but was thwarted not only by the way he had the reins twined around his right arm, but also because he had left his Colt back at the bunkhouse.

"Draw rein or I'll shoot!"

Slocum stood and tugged on the reins. It didn't take much persuading to convince the horses to cease their pulling.

"Get down. Get down or I'll drill you, I swear!"

Slocum saw how the road agent swung his six-gun around wildly.

"You new at this?"

"Shut up. Don't give me no backtalk or I'll kill you. I swear I will!"

Slocum knew the sound of a man talking himself into doing something. He silently fixed the reins and jumped down.

"You drop your gun," the road agent ordered.

"I'm not packing," Slocum said, turning first left and then right to show the outlaw.

"What's that on your arm?"

"Bandage." Slocum held up his left arm the best he could.

"Oh, yeah, I see now. Get over there."

"All I've got in the wagon are supplies. No gold. I'm driving *back* to the mine."

"Shut up, shut up!" The road agent was almost screaming. When the robber cocked his six-shooter, Slocum did as he was told and backed away. As het up as the owlhoot was, he might shoot an unarmed man in the back. If he started throwing lead, Slocum wanted to see it so he could maybe dodge.

The masked robber came up and started to climb into the driver's box. Slocum moved like lightning, crossing the distance between them, reaching up and grabbing the man's gun belt, and pulling hard. The man flew through the air and landed in the road, but he still clung to his six-gun. He fired at Slocum. Slocum straightened, felt pain lance through his head, and then the world went black.

12

Slocum was footsore by the time he got back to the mine. Most of the miners were in the mess hall. The clatter of spoons and forks and tin plates mingled with boisterous laughter as they blew off a little steam after a hard day deep underground. Slocum ignored them and headed directly for the office perched on its hill, where a single light still gleamed in the window.

Knocking on the door, Slocum waited until he heard a gruff, "Come on in. Door's always unlocked."

Entering, Slocum saw Morgan Haining at his desk. The man looked gaunt and on edge, but he pushed aside the stacks of paper to peer at Slocum. He adjusted the small lamp on the desk beside him, giving them more light.

"Good God, man, you look a fright. What's happened to you now?"

"Robbed," Slocum said, sitting heavily in the chair opposite Haining. He had held up well all day, but it felt as if all his energy vanished in a rush now that he had told the mine owner.

"Going to town or returning?" Haining sucked in his breath and held it. Slocum knew why. He gave him the bad news.

"On the way back. One road agent, but he got the drop

on me. I hadn't taken along a six-shooter or a rifle, not that it would have mattered much."

"Your arm. How you could drive the wagon was something of a mystery to me when Lucas told me he'd sent you."

"I don't think the robber did this as a rule. He was mighty edgy."

"Bad times in Cripple Creek. There's a passel of gold being taken from the mines but so little of it makes its way down to the ordinary citizen."

"It did this time. Worse, he drove off in the wagon."

"We have another," Haining said, "but you're right. This reduces the amount of ore we can haul to the mill by half."

"How long before you have the other wagon fixed?" Slocum asked.

"Fixed? What do you mean? It's broken down?"

"I thought so." Slocum hesitated, then changed what he was going to say. "Isn't its axle cracked?"

"I'll have to find out, but I am sure I saw it return from the mill just before sundown. No one mentioned anything about it being out of service."

"Must have been wrong," Slocum said, thinking about Herk and Singer lugging the heavy axle out of the wheel-wright's shop.

"It's tragedy enough losing those supplies. I can ill afford to buy more, but I must. And use the remaining wagon for the supplies rather than in hauling ore tomorrow."

"I'm pretty fair at tracking. Give me a horse and I'll find the robber before sunrise." Slocum tasted bile on his tongue when he made the request. When he had ridden into Cripple Creek, he'd been the owner of a good horse.

"No, you'll do nothing of the sort. This is a matter for the law. When you go into Cripple Creek in the morning, you'll notify the marshal and let him handle this."

"Folks in town don't think much of the marshal," Slocum said.

"Who ever does?" Haining smiled weakly. "That's the

nature of the beast, I suppose. He arrests them when they're getting drunk and having fun. No, you will notify him and not do anything as foolish as tracking down this desperado."

Slocum wasn't sure the road agent was that big a desperado but said nothing. He was too tired to do much more than find his bunk and turn in for the night.

He had left Haining to his work, found the trail in the dark, and started down it when he heard someone call his name. Slocum froze, again wishing he had his trusty Colt Navy at his hip.

"John?" This time the voice was softer, more feminine.

He turned, expecting to see Evangeline Haining. His eyebrows rose when her mother came from the shadows. Even in the dim light cast by the stars above, it was easy to see where the younger woman got her beauty. Darleen Haining was in her early forties, moved with the easy grace of a hunting mountain lion, and stopped just a few feet away. Slocum caught the scent of her seductive perfume and couldn't help staring at her cleavage. She wore her blouse with the top three buttons unfastened, giving a clear view of firm, white breasts.

"Good evening, Mrs. Haining," he said.

"We've never been formally introduced, but—"

"I've seen you around the office," Slocum said. "You obviously took the time to learn my name." He wanted to say more but wondered why she had stopped him, unless it had to do with her daughter.

"Why, yes, I asked after you. It's not often a man such as yourself comes to work at the Low Down."

Slocum still had no idea what she wanted. Her words could mean anything. He kept quiet, knowing she would eventually get around to telling him why she bothered to speak to him rather than letting her husband do so.

"You're quite the hero. Saving men like you did. And that terrible accident." She reached out gingerly and brushed her fingers along his bandaged forearm. For a moment Slocum thought she was going to let those fingers work on up to unbandaged arm. But she drew back.

"It's been a long day, ma'am. Mind if we continue this conversation later?"

"It won't take long," she said, stepping even closer. Slocum felt the heat from her lush body and again had the feeling she wanted to do more. Kiss him?

"I want to know what you said to my husband. Just now. Before you came out of the office."

"Why don't you ask him?"

"Because I'm asking you, John," she said. Her hand stroked over his stubbled cheek and lingered for a moment on his chin before slipping away like a thief in the night.

"I was robbed on the way back from town. Mr. Haining wants me to go back in the morning, tell the marshal, and then get more supplies."

"Robbed?" Darleen Haining's tone changed. "Why were you robbed?"

"He had a six-shooter and I didn't," Slocum said, thinking that was a strange question to ask. Why did any man rob another?

"The week's supplies are all gone?"

"Reckon so, unless the marshal can track the man down and find them. The road agent lit out with the wagon and everything in it."

"The wagon?" Now Darleen Haining's words carried midwinter frost with them. "You let the wagon be stolen?"

"Can't say I allowed it," Slocum said, resenting the implication that he was a party to the theft. "I wasn't armed and he had the drop on me. You'd prefer I'd ended up dead trying to stop the road agent?"

"You could have—" She cut off her words, stepped back, and glared at him, then swung around and flounced off, leaving Slocum alone on the path. He heard her skirts softly whispering long after she disappeared from sight. Only her pungent perfume remained to remind him she had been there. Slocum tried to figure out what that was all about but couldn't. He went directly to the bunkhouse and turned in, but his sleep was disturbed by odd dreams of Darleen Haining and Lucas Miles pointing at him, accusing him of some unknown crime—and then shooting him.

Ira Randolph sat silently beside Slocum on the wagon's hard seat. The young miner looked around apprehensively, knowing he was along to keep Slocum from being robbed again. But Miles had neglected to give Ira a weapon and Slocum had left his own six-gun back at the bunkhouse when he found out that Ira could not drive a rig.

They reached Cripple Creek without incident, but Slocum hadn't thought there would be trouble on the way into town. Who would want to steal an empty wagon? He pulled up in front of the marshal's office, secured the reins, and jumped down.

"Be back in a flash," he told Ira. The young man nodded and looked even more uneasy that Slocum was abandoning him to guard the wagon by himself.

Slocum went into the small office and found the marshal sitting at a small desk, whittling at a piece of pinewood. Shavings went everywhere as the lawman worked furiously on it.

"You Marshal Young?"

"Nope." The man kept whittling. Slocum went closer and peered at the badge pinned on his tattered vest.

"Then you're his deputy."

"Yep."

"Talkative cuss, aren't you?" This brought the deputy's head up from his work. He glared at Slocum as if he had just announced he was going to rob the bank.

"I ain't got time for the likes of you. You a miner?"

"Right now I'm a citizen that's been robbed."

"You and every other miner that's ever come to Cripple Creek. What is it? Cheated at a poker game?"

Slocum started to say something about that, then decided it would only muddy the water. He positioned himself directly across from the deputy so the man had to look at him if he ever took his eyes off the piece of wood he attacked with such zest.

"I was taking a load of supplies to the Low Down yesterday afternoon when a road agent held me up. Stole the supplies and the wagon."

"The Low Down? That's the one Morgan Haining owns, ain't it?"

"The supplies and wagon belong to Mr. Haining," Slocum said. "He'd be real grateful to get it all back. Barring that, he would probably give a reward to whoever caught the robber."

"Where'd it happen? On the road to the mine?"

"A couple miles outside Cripple Creek," Slocum said, getting angry.

"Ain't our concern. Marshal Young's the town marshal, not a federal marshal. You want to report this to the Teller County sheriff."

"Where's he?"

"Don't know. Maybe Florissant. Or Divide. Might even be at Victor. He gets around."

"And you don't give a damn."

"Nope."

"Where's Marshal Young?"

The deputy looked up and started to say that he didn't know and didn't care. The fire in Slocum's eyes made him recoil and drop his pinewood. He moved the pocketknife around as if this might keep Slocum at bay.

"H-he's down at the Oriental. Th-there's been some trouble there."

Slocum left without saying another word. He didn't trust himself to.

"We'll get the supplies, then I'll find the marshal," Slocum said to Ira as he clambered into the driver's box. His arm hurt and he was furious at the deputy, but there was nothing to do about the lawman that would matter. He would get the replacement supplies and then find Marshal Young. Somehow, he doubted the marshal was likely to be any more accommodating.

The shopkeeper was throwing out a dustpan full of dirt as Slocum drove up.

"Howdy," Slocum called. "Doubt you expected to see me back so quick."

"I heard what happened. News travels fast."

"You didn't hear it from the law in this town, did you?" Slocum said. "This is Ira. He'll help load up more supplies."

The shopkeeper pursed his lips and then mumbled to himself. Louder, he said, "I need some money first. The bill's gettin' mighty big for Low Down supplies. Mr. Haining doesn't have to pay it all, just some. A hundred, maybe?"

"Hunnerd dollars?" gasped Ira Randolph. To the young man, that was a princely sum.

"He's got to pay somethin'," the shopkeeper insisted. "It was bad you gettin' robbed and all, but that's not my problem. Keepin' my bills paid is."

"I need to talk to the marshal," Slocum said. "Where can I find him? After we're done, we'll head on back to the mine and see what Mr. Haining can do about settling the bill."

"Marshal Young's not due back into town 'fore sunset. He's been out serving process for Judge Quintero. Leastways, that's what he said he was gonna do today."

"The deputy said he was at the Oriental."

"Was," the storekeeper said, "but I seen him ride on out with my own eyes not a half hour ago. He didn't have much in the way of trail gear, so I figure he'll be back before sunup tomorrow."

Slocum was tossed on the horns of a dilemma. If he waited for the marshal, it would be dark and the trip back to the mine would be doubly dangerous—and there wouldn't be any supplies. But if he drove back to the Low Down with Ira right now to explain the situation to Morgan Haining, he wouldn't have either the supplies or a chance to file a grievance with Marshal Young.

"Ira, can you get the wagon back all by yourself? You

saw how I drove it. I need you to get back and tell Mr. Haining what's going on." The young man looked as if he would rather face a grizzly bear, but he nodded.

"He don't talk much, does he?"

"I'll write things down so he won't have to go into too much for Mr. Haining," Slocum said. "That suit you, Ira?" The young miner's head bobbed up and down furiously. "I can put in it how much you need to settle accounts, too," Slocum told the shopkeeper.

"In full?" The store owner's eyes lit up, and a broad grin split his face. "That'd be right nice, if he could pay it off in full. Clean slate and all. I'll be more 'n happy to give you a piece of paper and a pencil."

In the note, Slocum detailed everything that was needed and how he had stayed in Cripple Creek to speak with the marshal. He signed it and gave the sheet to Ira.

"Go back to the mine, then return in the morning for the supplies. You can pick me up then."

Ira's head bobbed some more. Slocum slapped him on the shoulder and let him rattle off. He doubted Ira would have any trouble with the team. They were feistier than the stolen horses, but not by much. They were used to pulling heavy loads, not racing the wind like young stallions.

"The marshal's first call when he gets into town is the Oriental," the merchant said. "Wets his whistle before he has to deal with your like. Claims it's to keep the rowdies from tearin' the joint up, but he gets free likker from the owner."

"Then I'll be waiting for him," Slocum said. He went around the building into the street and saw Ira sitting pleased as punch in the driver's box, reins in hand and moving the team along in a sprightly fashion. With luck, Ira would be back at about this time tomorrow so they could leave with more supplies, and the marshal would send along a deputy to guard them.

Slocum wondered if the man in the marshal's office would be worth a damn and knew the answer. But the rumor of an armed guard with them would scare off novices like the one who had stolen the other wagonload of goods.

Not having much money, Slocum had to loiter more than drink in the saloon, but he still had a few coins left in his vest pocket when the lawman came straggling in. The sun was setting, and Marshal Young looked about like Slocum felt.

"Whiskey, and none of that tarantula juice you usually serve. I been shot at and need to brace my nerves for what's coming tonight." The marshal had just knocked back his drink when Slocum accosted him with his story.

"So," the marshal said, after Slocum had completed his tale of theft, "you want me to leave town and go hunting for this fellow who wore a mask and might be a hundred miles away."

"He didn't get that far with a broke-down team like the one hitched to the wagon."

"I'll see what I can do, but it's got to be tomorrow," the marshal said. "Tonight's going to be one gullywhumper."

"Why's that?" Slocum asked. He swung around when gunfire outside drowned out his question.

"That's why," Marshal Young said. "Got boys from the Molly Magee Mine and the Lost Friend itchin' to mix it up. The feud's been buildin' for nigh on a month. Full moon tonight's the perfect time for them to get drunk and do somethin' I won't like." More gunfire echoed through the saloon. The marshal hitched up his gun belt, settled himself with another quick drink, then marched out. Slocum followed, remaining just inside the doorway. Not for the first time he wished he had his own six-shooter strapped on his hip.

In the street, a couple dozen men squared off. Two fired their six-guns in the air, and the rest were armed with ax handles and anything else convenient to bash their enemies over the head with.

"Boys, I don't mind if you whale away on each other with your bare knuckles, but you put down them six-shooters and drop the barrel staves. You hear me?"

"Go to hell, Marshal!" one of the miners shouted.

The lawman ducked as a rock sailed through the air. Slocum watched it sail past and break a coal oil lamp in a wall sconce.

"Fire!" the barkeep yelled. "Those bastards set fire to my saloon!"

Slocum saw the man wasn't far wrong. The broken reservoir trickled kerosene down the wall like a fuse. Fire licked down, threatening to set the place ablaze.

He moved almost as fast as the barkeep to put out the fire before it got a foothold on the dry wood in the wall and floor. The bartender used his apron to beat out the flames on the wall, and Slocum stamped out the few tiny hot spots threatening to take hold on the floor.

Outside he heard a full-fledged riot in progress. Marshal Young shouted and men screamed in anger.

"Thanks," the barkeep said. "If a fire ever got started, this whole damned town would go up."

Barely had the words left his mouth when a kerosene lamp smashed through the window, sending glass splinters everywhere. Slocum turned from it, shielding his face with his arm against a blast of heat that staggered him. The spilled kerosene had spread and ignited in the blink of an eye.

"Fire! The saloon's on fire!" shouted the barkeep. This time he didn't try to put it out, because it had already spread too far, too fast. The bartender burst out into the street, leaving Slocum inside, the fire rising up all around him.

Trapped!

13

The flames scorched Slocum's eyebrows. He threw up his arm to protect his face, but the heat made the bandage on his forearm begin to smolder. Turning, he hunted frantically for a way out of the saloon. He saw part of the side wall sag as the heat boiled off the whitewash, and he took a chance. Lowering his head like a charging bull, he ran flat out as hard as he could for the wall. He ducked his head at the last instant and hit the wall with his shoulder. The flimsy wood gave way and spilled him out into the alley beside the saloon. He landed hard, realized his clothing was on fire, and started rolling in the dirt. By the time he had put out the fires on his shirt and pants, he was in the middle of the main street.

Sitting up, he saw furious activity all around. In the distance a fire bell clanged, and a team of neighing horses pulled a fire engine with a pump on it from the other side of town. Slocum wasn't sure what happened, but someone picked him up bodily and threw him across the street, as if he were nothing more than a piece of debris.

He hit the ground hard again but scrambled to his feet. The heat from the burning saloon caused him to squint. Flames leaped outward from the windows and threatened to engulf the buildings on either side. A boomtown like

Cripple Creek was built quick and with no regard to preventing the spread of such a fire. If the two buildings on either side of the saloon went up, more would follow until the entire town was engulfed.

"What can I do?" he asked the wizened old man who wore a fire hat with a gold badge on it proclaiming him to be captain of the volunteers.

The man's rheumy eyes took in Slocum, then he pointed. "Pump. You oughta be up fer that, even with a bad arm."

Slocum didn't wait to get more instructions. The rocker arm on the pump was hard to move, so another man joined him. Then two more, on the other side of the pump arm. In unison they began pushing and pulling, getting the balky equipment working. At first the spray of water from the storage tank on the fire engine was weak, hardly more than a single drunk pissing on the fire to put it out. After several hard up and down circuits, Slocum felt the suction begin. A steady stream of water launched then, arching high into the evening sky and falling directly onto the saloon roof.

It was backbreaking work, especially doing it one-handed, but Slocum never slowed. The other men tired and were replaced, but he kept going until he was soaked from the spray and black from the soot. Finally, the captain yelled in Slocum's ear, "Stop pumpin'. Ain't no more water. Ain't no more fire, neither."

Slocum took a couple steps back and looked around. He had been so focused on the pumping he had not paid attention to anything else. The saloon was a loss, as were the buildings on either side. But they were only partially in ruin. The roofs had fallen in but their walls remained. And the rest of Cripple Creek was safe from fire. This time.

"Did the marshal catch the son of a bitch who threw the coal oil lamp into the Oriental?"

The fire captain took off his hat and scratched his head.

"Damned if I know. I hope so since I want to be the one to fit a noose 'round his filthy neck." With that the man tossed his hat into the driver's box, climbed up painfully, and barked orders to the driver to get them back to the barn where the engine was kept.

Slocum sat on the boardwalk across from the destroyed saloon and simply stared. His right arm ached, and his face was blistered from the heat. But he was alive.

"You did the work of five men," he heard a familiar voice say. Slocum looked over his shoulder to see the shopkeeper.

"I did what I could."

"It was mighty good, I'd say. You need a place to sleep? Want some vittles? The missus fixes decent roast."

The offer was too tempting to pass up.

"Goes against my better judgment," the shopkeeper said, "but I reckon you earned a little more credit for the mine."

"Much obliged," Slocum said. "For everything." The merchant hadn't received the full payment as Slocum had hoped he would. Morgan Haining probably didn't have that much in gold, but Ira Randolph and his father had returned with about half the amount owed by the Low Down.

"Get on back to the mine," the shopkeeper growled. "Dig out a ton of gold and pay me in full next time."

Slocum sat back as the elder Randolph handled the team on the fully laden wagon.

"Looks like fire," Randolph said.

"Could have been worse," Slocum allowed. His right arm still ached and his left was filthy with soot. And in spite of a decent night's sleep, he was still dog tired, but he felt good about all that he had done in town. "What's happening at the mine?"

"Mr. Haining is upset," Randolph said. "Wagon needed to move ore to crusher."

Bit by bit Slocum got the story from the speech-impaired Randolphs. Haining needed this wagon desperately to move the high-grade ore coming out of the Low Down to the crusher and smelter. But the supplies were also needed to keep the miners working.

Slocum curled up atop the supplies and dozed as they

made their way back. Only when Randolph pulled up and the rocking motion stopped did Slocum snap awake. But he would have anyway because of the foreman's shouts.

"You lazy sons of bitches, get the wagon unloaded. We got a load of ore to get down into the valley pronto."

Slocum hopped off and tried to help the two Randolphs unload the wagon, but both of his arms bothered him.

"Slocum," said Miles, "you look like something the cat drug in. You able to swing a pick yet?"

"Doubt it," Slocum said. He held up his arms. His right was swollen, and the left looked worse than it was, due to the filthy bandage. The blisters on his face added to the pathetic picture.

"I'd fire you, but the boss said no. You drive the ore wagon. That way we don't lose no able-bodied man from down below."

Slocum nodded. He continued to do what he could to help unload but only got in the way. He contented himself with soaking his face and right arm in the rain barrel beside the cookhouse until the pain receded and he felt almost human. Stripping off his bandage, he washed it out and gingerly reapplied it to his arm. The cut hidden by the bandage was starting to heal, but it itched now. The cool water and clean bandage made it feel almost whole.

"Move your ass, Slocum!" Miles barked. "I want two loads of ore down to the smelter today. More! Time's a'wastin'!"

Slocum climbed in and gripped the reins the best he could. Only long years of experience allowed him to get the team moving. He pulled over to the mouth of the mine shaft and let the men fill the bed with the heavy ore. Even in this form, Slocum could see the value of the rock being pulled out. Color sparkled everywhere in the quartz. The assay might prove to be on the low side, he figured.

"G'wan, get outta here!" shouted the miner in charge of the loading. "And get back here pronto. We kin do what Miles wants, two loads, if you shake your tail."

Slocum waved to the man, who grinned in response,

then concentrated on using both hands to get the team pulling. His arms hurt, but he found that the longer he drove, the better he felt. Guiding the team down the narrow road to the larger one leading into the valley where the crusher, mill, and smelter were, Slocum found himself drifting along. His mind turned over myriad ideas, but he wasn't coming to any conclusions.

He knew Miles had to be mixed up in the high-grading scheme and suspected Herk and Singer, too. The silver concha he still carried in his pocket pointed to Herk being the one who had murdered Thompson and Bowden. For all he knew, Herk might also have been responsible for cutting the ropes lowering the elevator that had given Slocum his game arm and had killed Billy. But what of Darleen Haining? Slocum tried to figure her out and couldn't.

Thinking of her caused him to pleasantly dwell on her daughter and their times together.

An hour later, after daydreaming mostly of Evangeline, he drew up near the side of the crusher where ore was shoveled onto a belt that took it to grinding rollers where it was pulverized into gravel-sized chunks. From there it went to a mill that produced finer pebbles, almost dust. This went into the smelter to separate the gold from the dross.

Slocum hopped down and let the mill foreman get his men to work.

"Don't recognize you," the foreman said. "You work for Haining?"

"This is all Low Down Mine ore," Slocum said.

"Reckoned it might be."

Slocum and the foreman talked idly, then Slocum asked, "How often does an axle break on one of these wagons?"

"Axle? Not all that often. Wheels give out sooner," the foreman said. "You don't look like the worrying kind. Why the interest?"

"I was wondering why men from the Low Down would buy an extra axle in town."

"This one's in good condition. Might be the other wagon that's got problems, though it's been rolling along real sprightly. Ah, hell." The foreman let out a shout and left Slocum abruptly as he went to chew out one of his workers who had gotten his sleeve caught in the gears. This gave Slocum the chance to wonder about that other wagon. He decided the foreman must mean the one that Slocum had gotten stolen out from under him, though that wagon had been in good condition.

Seeing Herk and Singer with the spare axle was a mystery he had no ready answer for.

The foreman returned, shaking his head and grumbling. "I do declare, if their heads weren't sewn on, they'd lose them. I told them a hundred times to watch out with their sleeves and pants when working near the equipment. Do they listen? I'd let the son of a gun go through the crusher 'cept it'd get blood on the ore."

Slocum had to laugh.

"My own boss'll be chewing nails and spitting tacks if I don't get a second load to you today."

"Third, you mean," the foreman said.

"Don't think I can get these nags to pull that fast."

"No, no, not you. I meant three loads from the Low Down." The foreman craned his neck and looked past the mill and squinted at the sun. "Might even get a fourth load."

Slocum started to laugh outright at such a notion, then wondered if there wasn't more to what the man said.

"There's been another load this morning?"

"Hours back," the foreman said.

Slocum considered this. Unless the stolen wagon had been recovered, the Low Down was running only one wagon, and Slocum was sitting on it.

"You sure it was ore from the Low Down Mine?"

"Sure as can be. Leastways, that's where the bill's going. Got to get back to work. You hurry up, hear? I got to keep these lazy galoots of mine working. Otherwise, they'll fall under the rollers when they nod off."

Slocum snapped the reins and moved the wagon around to a spot in the shade of a stand of cottonwoods some distance away. The horses were pleased at being able to crop the short grass growing there while Slocum sat and watched. Less than twenty minutes passed before another wagon rattled up. He sat up straighter and watched, then sagged. It was a load of ore from the Molly Magee. He recognized the driver.

"We've wasted enough time," Slocum said to his team, but he hesitated when he saw another wagon kicking up a dust cloud on its way to the mill. Slocum pulled down his hat to shade his eyes and waited for the dust to settle. A slow smile came to his lips. His time hadn't been wasted after all.

Slouched over in the driver's seat of the other wagon was Singer. And the wagon he drove wasn't the one stolen from Slocum on his way back from Cripple Creek. There hadn't been a third wagon in the Low Down camp, yet one of Miles's cronies drove this one. And from the mound of ore in the rear, it was loaded to within a few ounces of breaking an axle.

Singer walked around the wagon, keeping away from the men unloading. When the foreman came out with a handful of papers, Singer scribbled something on the bottom that might have been nothing more than an *X*, then jumped back into the wagon and took off when the wagon was empty. Slocum watched him depart in a hurry, knowing this was what the foreman had meant when he said the Low Down might deliver four wagonloads in a day.

Only the wagon Singer drove wasn't carrying Low Down ore. Not exactly.

Slocum figured out the mechanics of the situation. High-graded ore from the Low Down was dumped into the other wagon and brought for crushing and smelting. When the payoff for the gold came, Singer would accept delivery of the gold and take it back to his boss—Lucas Miles. If Singer happened to receive the payoff for all the gold delivered, both by himself and the driver from the Low Down, Miles would separate it and deliver to Morgan Haining only that which had been freighted down by a Low Down driver.

"The son of a bitch is making Haining pay for all the smelting. They steal his ore, make him pay for the smelting, and keep what would be a tidy profit."

Slocum knew following Singer wasn't going to be easy. Tracking a man in a wagon while driving another wagon was downright stupid. All Singer had to do was glance back and spot Slocum and the fur would fly. The one thing Slocum had going for him were the other mines bringing their loads to the mill. Singer might ignore anyone behind him, thinking the wagon belonged to the Molly Magee or some other concern.

But sooner or later Slocum would have to pass Singer. When he did, he was sure to be spotted. Hanging back as far as he could, hoping to see where Singer turned off the road, availed him little. The other man kicked up quite a dust cloud in his hurry to get back to wherever it was he had loaded the ore.

Then Slocum figured it all out.

The meandering mine tunnels Evangeline Haining had found went under the Low Down's most valuable vein. He had seen two men in the mine itself checking the content. From that point they high-graded the ore and just dumped it down the side of the mountain to the road, where Singer loaded it into the wagon. The tailings from that mine had vanished because the high-graders loaded everything that came out of the mine, possibly through carelessness or more likely because Miles didn't want any evidence of new work at that mine.

Slocum almost let out a whoop of glee when he saw Singer pull up beneath the mouth of the mine and wave to someone inside. Herk came out, wiped sweat off his forehead, and waved back. The huge man disappeared into the mine, then returned pushing an ore cart, which he tipped over. The contents tumbled down the mountainside, glittering in the afternoon sunlight.

"What should I do?" Slocum mused. He sucked on his teeth as he thought. Getting Marshal Young out here wasn't much of an answer. He had locked horns with the marshal's deputy and remembered the way he had been steered toward the county sheriff for any real law enforcement. Young might not be interested. Or he might be paid off by Miles and the others.

Slocum could tell Haining and drag him out here by force, if necessary, to convince him that his wife was wrong and that the Low Down had big problems with high-graders. Or he could round up a dozen miners and do a little law enforcing of his own. The Randolphs would join him. He knew others would, too, when he explained that not only their pay but future bonuses were being siphoned off by Miles and his henchmen.

That looked to be the best way of dealing with the problem. Slocum tugged down the brim of his hat and looked to one side as he drove past the pullout where Singer worked like a fiend to load the ore tossed down from above.

Slocum hit a rock in the road and felt the wagon slew under him. He slowed, chanced a look backward, and saw Singer staring at him. Slocum turned away, kept driving, and let out a sigh of relief when no alarm was raised.

He drove steadily, going higher into the hills, but his team tired quickly. Slocum reluctantly pulled to the side of the road to give his horses a brief rest. He rubbed his arms and stretched, trying to get his muscles to stop throbbing.

But as he sat in the wagon, he grew increasingly uneasy. During the war, he had relied on this sense to stay alive. As he turned, he saw a blur. Then the barrel of a six-shooter crashed into the side of his head. He tumbled out of the driver's seat, hitting the ground hard. He tried to rise, then collapsed, unconscious.

14

Slocum groaned and rolled onto his side. It took a few seconds to realize his hands were bound behind his back and that he lay with his head slightly downslope. Blinking his eyes, he tried to see around him. Panic surged when he thought he was blind. Then he realized he was in a very dark place, all light cut off.

"A mine," he muttered. Sucking in a deep breath, he recognized the usual smell of a mine shaft far underground. Scooting around scraped his shoulder but let him find a wall. Digging in his toes, he forced himself against the rocky wall and slowly sat up until his back was pressing into cold stone and his legs stretched in front of him.

He still couldn't see the tiniest glimmer of light anywhere. Slocum blinked a few more times to be sure his eyelids were working and that he wasn't caught in some horrible nightmare. Everything but sight told him he was alive and prisoner in a mine. The musty smell, the cold that made him shiver, the rough rock, the silence complete except for his own harsh breathing, all told him he had been knocked out and dumped into a mine.

His thoughts turned back to what had happened. He remembered watching Singer and was pretty sure he had seen Herk in the mouth of the mine where he and Evangeline had been earlier. But someone had sneaked up on him and swung a mean pistol. He had been buffaloed and unconscious before he could identify his assailant. Not that it mattered. He was in a jam and had to get out somehow.

Slocum twisted about, but getting his bound hands in front of him wasn't going to happen unless he dislocated his shoulders. He settled down, found a sharp outjut of rock, and began the tedious chore of sawing through the rope around his wrists. He nicked himself in the process, and his hands were slick with his own blood by the time the last strand parted.

He heaved a sigh of relief, rubbed his wrists, and felt the abrasions there. Nothing serious. His left forearm still hurt more than his other injuries. Slocum worked his fingers into his vest pocket and found the small tin holding his lucifers. He counted the matches. Only three.

Slocum struck one and held it high over his head, squinting to keep from being totally blinded. Even so, his eyes watered at the sudden flare. He got a good look around and saw that he was in the bottom of a shaft. Slocum's heart skipped a beat when he saw a corpse on the far side. The clothing had turned to dust and the flesh mummified, a testament to the pit having been used to get rid of other unwanted snoops.

Slocum moved his fingers down to the very end of the match as it burned. Two more and then he would be plunged into utter darkness again and have no chance of escaping unless he could do it by feel. He doubted that was possible. The dead body was mute testimony to that.

As the match burned to an end, Slocum dived forward and dropped it onto the dried sleeve of the corpse. It flared brilliantly and dazzled him for a moment, then settled down to a more manageable fire.

"A hell of a cooking fire," Slocum said, edging away. The mummified hand had caught fire, and ghoulish flames danced off each fingertip. Seeing that even this source of fuel wasn't going to last long, Slocum turned his attention to the walls. He was truly caught in the bottom of a pit. Slocum peered up and realized the full horror of his situation. The sides of the pit were jagged, but there was no way his injuries would allow him to climb out, even if he could find handholds and spots to use as steps.

Slocum paced the bottom of the pit, skirting the burning body, hunting for something to use to get out. There was a pile of rope at one side, but it was hardly long enough to be of much use from this deep in the pit. The surface flaked off when he ran his hand over it, but the core of the rope had remained intact against the elements all this time. A few rusted pulley wheels showed that a hoist had once stretched across the top of the pit. But even if the timber was still there, he had no way of reaching it and only fifteen feet of rope to throw over it.

Worse, he couldn't climb up a rope to the top with his arms still weak from cuts and burns.

Heaving a deep sigh, Slocum continued his examination and came to the conclusion he was truly trapped. Nothing else on the floor of the pit would aid him, and he couldn't climb the sides. The greasy black smoke from the burning body began to choke him. Not sure what else to do, he took the rope and fastened one end around his chest. That left about twelve feet free. And he still came up short, even if he could have seen somewhere above him to lasso.

"Thirst," Slocum said. He swung about so fast that the cloying smoke followed him like a slow-witted dog chasing its master. He saw the seepage on the wall and remembered the underground river that had carried him into the lower mine—the mine shaft where the high-graders stole Haining's ore.

He used a rusted pulley to chip at the rock and get a sliver removed. A flow of water about the size of his little finger poured from the wall. The leakage slowed and finally stopped. Gasping for breath, Slocum doubled his effort with the rusty pulley wheel, finding a sharp edge and using it on the same spot he had attacked before until he got a steady flow back. Then he hammered as hard as he could until the rock shattered. Slocum was knocked backward by a geyser jetting from the wall.

Sputtering, he fought to keep his head above water. In spite of the gushing water, the corpse continued to burn, floating on the surface and following him upward. The thick black smoke continued to burn his eyes and lungs, but the light from the burning hand was enough to show him the way out. He floated up within six feet of the lip of the pit. Arched over it stretched the hoist support that had once held both rope and pulleys. Slocum let out a cheer. He could get out. The water would carry him up and over the top any instant now.

But it didn't. The water had stopped rising. He thrashed around and tried to reach the lip of the pit some feet above, but his wet hands failed to give him purchase. His fingers slid off repeatedly. And then Slocum felt the water level going back down. The water was somehow draining from the pit.

The pit had been dry when he had been tossed into it. Any water that had seeped into it had drained faster than it accumulated, leaving the corpse dry enough to burn. Slocum flopped over in the water and saw only one finger of the mummified hand continuing to burn.

It was the middle finger.

This made him furious. He surged upward again and clawed at the edge of the pit, only to flop back into the water. He got tangled in the rope he had fastened around himself.

"Rope!"

He had worked more than one range in his day. Roping cattle was always challenging but was something he was expert at. As the light from the burning hand faded, he judged the distance to the timber above the pit and let fly with the rope. He had only one chance before he was once more plunged into stygian dark.

The rope sailed upward and looped over the beam. The

free end came back toward him as the light snuffed out. Slocum grabbed where the rope must be hanging and missed it, but heard it swishing in the air. He caught it as it swung back toward him. Hauling hard, he felt the bite of the rope under his armpits. Arms burning like those of the ignited corpse, he pulled hard and heaved himself out of the water. Panting, he paused to recover strength and felt the water draining faster under him. This was his only chance. The desperation born of that thought gave him more strength.

In darkness blacker than any midnight, Slocum climbed. The rope began to abrade and yield. He felt it slipping as strand after strand of the old decayed rope parted under his weight. He became more determined than ever. He would not end up at the bottom of the pit, waiting to die and become a torch for some other son of a bitch thrown down there to die.

He banged his head hard enough to jar him. In his frantic, dazed state he didn't immediately understand what had happened. Then he did. He had pulled himself up so far that his head hit the beam over the pit. Reaching up with a shaking left hand, he felt the splintery timber. He reached around it, got his upper arm over the beam, and then heaved with what strength remained in him. He got both arms over the beam, then pulled up and locked his feet around it.

Slocum thought he could stay like that forever, but the way the wood began creaking and yielding under his weight told him he had to move. Fast. Not knowing which way to go was no problem. Either side of the pit would be safer than dangling under the beam if it broke. Splinters cutting into his flesh, he went hand over hand until he found a support. Awkwardly looping his rope around the top beam as if he were tethering a horse, he relied on this safety line to hold his weight for a few seconds as he grasped the vertical support.

Slocum swung around, untangled the rope, and felt his

feet touch solid rock. He was out of the pit. Sudden weakness hit him like a sledgehammer blow. He sank to the floor and trembled from the strain and the knowledge that he was still alive. When he recovered, he sat up and pressed out his wet clothing. The only sounds he heard now were the slow drip-drip-drip off his clothing and the sloshing of the water as it drained from the pit. Slocum took out his tin once more and considered using his final two lucifers. Deciding he had no choice, hoping the water had been kept out of the usually airtight box, he took out a lucifer and scratched it against the mine wall.

Nothing. Water had ruined it.

The remaining match felt dry under his fingers, but he couldn't be sure. He struck this one and was rewarded with a sputtering flame. But he knew the match wouldn't burn very long since his wet fingers had dampened the matchstick. Slocum took a quick look around and jumped like a goosed toad when he saw a ledge above him lined with miner's candles. He wasted no time getting to his feet and grabbing one. The wick sputtered and finally lit before the lucifer gasped its last and died amid a crackling shower of blue-and-yellow sparks. Slocum thrust the wicks of two more candles into the flame of the first and enjoyed a veritable flood of light. He walked back to the pit and looked in.

He realized how lucky he had been when he studied the timber. The beam that he had used to escape was almost broken in half after holding his weight for only a few seconds. As it was, the wood had lasted long enough to allow him to escape the pit. Holding one candle out cast wan light downward. The water below him was dark and sinking fast. He couldn't even make out where the water had flowed into the pit.

And it no longer mattered. He had escaped.

"Thanks," he said, quietly paying tribute to the unknown man whose mummified corpse had given him enough light to begin his escape.

Slocum filled his pockets with candles from the ledge and saw that he could not get around the pit and explore the mine in that direction. He turned and went in the opposite direction, that being as good as the other, since he had no idea where he was or how he might find the exit.

Holding the candle out, his hand shaking and still not recovered from the strain, Slocum tried to find any vagrant air current that would direct him out of the mine. He followed the drift around, trying to get a sense of how far underground he was and how long the mine had been abandoned.

From the look of them, no one had worked the tunnels in years. These might be some of the earliest diggings in the Cripple Creek district, exploited and abandoned. But there was no clue how to get out of the middle of the mountain.

Slocum trooped along for a while, then slowed and finally stopped. Other than his own harsh breathing and the crackle from the miner's candle in his hand, there had been no sound at all. He pressed his ear against a rock wall and strained to hear what might have been an animal crying in pain. He came to a juncture and listened hard, taking a route away from where he "felt" the way out must be. The sound grew louder, and he finally recognized it.

A woman was crying. Sobbing. Trying to hold in her emotions and failing.

He advanced slowly, not sure what he was getting himself into. A sudden widening in the drift showed a large chamber like the ones bored into the Low Down Mine to provide a staging area for miners and equipment next to the elevator.

Crazy, dark shadows danced off the vaulted roof and curved walls. But Slocum saw the source of the sounds right away.

"Evie!"

"J-John? Is it really you? You found me! I never thought that you'd come. Th-that anyone would. Could. Oh!" Evangeline Haining broke out crying now. He hurried to her side and saw how she was tied. Her hands had been fastened behind her and a double loop of new rope circled her ankles, then ran over to a rusty ore cart. She was tied and secured to keep her from getting away.

"Who did this?"

"I . . . I don't know. It must have been Miles, but I never saw. Somebody grabbed me last night before I went to bed. They put a sack over my head and bounced me all around. I passed out or they hit me. Oh, I don't know what happened!"

"You woke up in the mine?"

"I figured it out. It was completely dark so I had to guess, but it wasn't hard." She craned her head around. "I thought that was an ore cart. I was right."

He fumbled getting her bonds off. When he finished, she threw her arms around his neck and cried into his shoulder. Evangeline fought for control, sniffed, and pushed away from him.

"You're wet," she said. "Your clothes are drenched."

"I went for a swim," Slocum said. "I was knocked out on my way back for another load of ore for the mill. I ended up in what turned into a well."

She looked at him curiously. A glint came to her eyes and she smiled. It wasn't a shy smile.

"You're wet," she repeated.

"So?"

"So am I," Evangeline said, moving back into the circle of his arms. "Is that so strange? I've been tied up and was sure my life was forfeit, and now you rescue me and . . . I want you!"

Her lips crushed Slocum's. He returned the passion. Her reaction wasn't all that outrageous since he shared it, too. Something about almost dying made him—and Evangeline—horny as hell.

His fingers stroked through her tangled hair, then moved lower, down her back and to her skirt. He bunched up the cloth until he could work his hand underneath and find warm flesh. Her thigh throbbed with life. She twisted slightly so his hand slid around between her legs. He found what she'd meant when she'd said she was wet. Her inner legs were slick with her inner juices leaking from her aroused sex.

His hand moved up and a finger slid easily into her. The woman moaned and ground herself down into his hand. Her mouth worked fiercely against his and then her tongue snaked out, pushing past his lips and going boldly into his mouth. Slocum's tongue began an erotic dance that frolicked from his mouth to hers and back, slipping and sliding and stroking over her tongue until they both gasped with need.

"Take me, John. Take me. Don't be gentle. I need you inside me. Now!"

She hiked up her own skirts and exposed herself. It took Slocum a little longer to drop his jeans and get free, but when he did he felt her hot hand circle him and draw him toward her hot, moist channel.

"The candle," he muttered. "Must be sure it doesn't go out."

"I'm hot enough to light it again. We both are," she said. Slocum cast a quick glance in the direction of the miner's candle burning where he had placed it on the ore cart. It would last long enough, and he needn't worry about starting another candle yet.

"Now, John, don't stop. Go fast, as fast as you can. Burn me up!"

Evangeline lifted a leg and wrapped it around his waist, drawing her crotch into his. His meaty shaft sank easily into her, taking away their breaths. Slocum was surrounded by tight, clinging female flesh. Evie tensed and relaxed, giving him an added thrill. He ran his hands around her back and down until he cupped her buttocks. He lifted her easily and swung her about. He deposited her on the edge of the ore cart, her legs dangling down on either side of his body.

The woman leaned back and rammed herself down hard around his impaling manhood. She began lifting and twisting, moving to get the most stimulation possible out of their coupling. For Slocum it was pure torture. She teased and tormented and slipped up and down his length until he could hardly restrain himself.

"Hard, John," she repeated. "Take me hard and fast. I want it. Oh, how I want to feel alive!"

He began stroking back and forth with powerful movements of his hips. He slammed hard into Evangeline, ground down and then pulled back as fast as he had entered. She gasped and sobbed again, this time in unbridled ecstasy. Slocum pistoned faster into her tightness and felt the heat mounting. Carnal friction threatened to burn him to a stub. He worked his hips faster.

"Yes, yes!" she cried out. Evangeline arched her back, threw her head back, and collapsed all around Slocum's hidden length. As her climax eased, Slocum began stroking even faster. He had to. His loins were on fire. The white-hot tide rose within him and then erupted uncontrollably.

Evangeline gasped again and clawed at his shoulders until the winds of ecstasy died down to a mere warm afterglow.

"Thank you, John. That was what I needed."

"Me, too," he said. "It was almost worth nearly dying to get this chance."

"Almost? Almost worth it? I'm still horny. I'll wear you down. I'll—"

"We have to get out of here, Evie," he reminded her. "As pleasant as this was, there are more pressing matters."

"This pressing into me is all I want," the woman said, fondling his flaccid length.

"Later. After we get out of here."

"That's a promise I'll hold you to," she said.

"Do you have any idea what mine we're in?" While she went down a list of possible locations, he lit a second candle from the one that had collapsed to a thin disk of wax on the edge of the ore cart. The new light highlighted Evangeline's face and made her seem even lovelier. That she hadn't bothered to pull down her skirt and was still wantonly exposed didn't do anything to take away from her beauty.

"So," she finished. "It seems we might be in a mine adjoining the one where we found the high-graders."

"I know Herk and Singer are involved in the theft of your pa's ore," Slocum said. "Miles is, too. I feel that in my gut."

"But?" Evangeline prodded. "You're not telling me something."

Slocum stayed silent. There had to be more to the high-grading than he had seen. Lucas Miles wasn't smart enough to have set up the operation on his own.

But before he worried more about who might be involved in the theft of the ore, he and Evangeline had to get out of this rocky prison. Looking around the large chamber didn't show him any obvious way out.

15

"That almost makes being kidnapped, tied up, and dumped in a mine worthwhile," Evangeline said, fluttering her skirt to get dust off it. Slocum watched. In the candlelight he saw the canyons and valleys he had just explored so ardently, but the edge was off now.

"We need to get out of here," Slocum said.

"I'm in no hurry. Not if more of that is in store," Evangeline said, glancing at his crotch. There was no action there, though, because Slocum had finished buttoning up and had started prowling the chamber like an animal in a cage.

He had thought he would find an easy way out. He quickly realized that wasn't going to happen. They were near an elevator shaft, but all the equipment had been removed. He could hardly see the speck of nighttime sky high above. He tried counting how many levels underground they were and stopped at eight. Climbing that high would be impossible without ropes—or a working elevator. Just thinking about getting out using a rope made his arms ache.

"No way we can go up, is there?" Evangeline's voice was small and weak as the realization that this wasn't a lark came to her.

"There might be ladders between levels. It depends on how long this mine was being operated."

"Right!" she said, brightening. "Papa always insists on drilling up to a higher level and putting ladders up in case of cave-ins."

"In the older drifts and stopes," Slocum said. Where he had worked in the Low Down was at the end of new tunnels. And most mine foremen ignored the chance of needing to get their miners out in favor of keeping work going along veins of ore. They considered such safety escapes a waste of time to build. And Slocum had to agree. Usually it was.

But he wanted to keep Evangeline from getting too despondent. There had to be a way out. Someone had brought them here, after all. If not by elevator, then there was another way in. He couldn't see why Miles or whoever had thrown him into the pit hadn't simply dropped him down this shaft. Such a fall would have killed him. It might not have afforded Miles the pleasure of thinking of his victim dying a slow death, but it would have been more effective. Slocum found his hands balled into fists thinking of Miles and his henchmen.

"How do you think they got you here?" Slocum asked.

"I don't know. I don't remember them lowering me, though."

"Then there's probably a way out on this level. They might not have even known of this old elevator shaft," Slocum said. He held his candle as high as he could, looking for some trace of a ladder down the side. There weren't even holes in the rock showing where such a way down into the mine had ever existed.

"If I can find the way back to the pit where they tossed me, the tunnel on the far side must lead out."

"It's good you didn't find it earlier," Evangeline said. He looked at her for a moment, then nodded. He would never have found her if he had discovered the way out. Lady Luck had ridden on his shoulder—and Evangeline's.

He hoped the run of luck wasn't at an end. Slocum wasn't sure how he had gotten to this chamber, since he had been following the sounds Evangeline had made, but backtracking might not be too difficult. His footprints in the dirt ought to provide an easy map back to the pit. From there, getting out of the mine shouldn't be difficult at all.

"You're looking as pleased as punch," Evangeline said.

"We can get out of here," he said with real assurance.

"Then let's do it. I want to be home by breakfast and get some food. I can't remember the last time I ate."

Slocum shook his head. Women were always practical. He hadn't noticed how his belly rubbed up against his backbone until she mentioned it. If anything, he was thirstier than he was hungry.

As if she read his mind, Evangeline said, "Could we get some water to drink from that pit? The underground river must be the one that supplies Cripple Creek with all its water."

"I wouldn't want to rely on it," Slocum said, remembering how the corpse had floated on the surface before vanishing back under the rising water. Dirt could be filtered out through his bandanna, but the corruption of a corpse—even a burned one—could kill them.

"Then let's get going."

"Look around for more candles," Slocum said. "I've got five left, and they've all been burned about halfway down."

"Hmm, eight hours of light?" Evangeline started a methodical hunt around the chamber and found two more candles. Slocum joined her, hoping to find a carbide lamp. It would provide twice the light and not require the transfer of flame from one candle to the next. He wished he had more lucifers, but he didn't.

"That's all we're going to get," Slocum said.

"Should we each have a lighted candle?" Evangeline asked.

Slocum didn't want to waste the candles, but relighting if his candle went out would be difficult if not impossible. He didn't cotton much to the idea of finding tinder and striking steel against a rock until a spark caught. That might take an hour or longer, depending on what he could find in the mine fumbling around in utter darkness.

He lit one of Evangeline's candles and saw this simple act let her relax a mite. Together they examined the five drifts branching off the main room. Slocum found his footprints in one and started down the drift, spirits high.

The longer he walked, the more he realized tracking in the dust wasn't going to be as easy as he had thought. Twice he went down wrong corridors only to retrace when he discovered the tracks he thought were his own had vanished.

"Are we lost, John?" Evangeline asked after he had stomped back to a juncture.

"We know where we are," he said, a touch of bitterness in his words. "What we need to know is where we want to be."

Evangeline found this funny and laughed. Before Slocum could say anything, she suddenly clamped her hand over her mouth and turned to him. Her eyes were wide and frightened.

"What's wrong?"

"Do you hear them?"

"Who?" Slocum cocked his head to one side and listened hard. At first he thought she was imagining things. The mine was as silent as a tomb—as their tomb, if he didn't find a way out. But before he could say anything, he heard the voices. Distant. Soft. Muffled. But voices.

"We're not alone," he said.

"W-we might be, John. There's no sign of anything else alive here."

"What are you getting at?"

"The voices. They might be tommyknockers."

"Who's that? Somebody who works at the mine?"

"Not who, what. The spirits of dead miners. The poor souls who are killed underground go into the rock."

Slocum snorted in disgust. He didn't have time for such superstition. But he heard the voices again. They got louder and he almost made out distinct words. It wasn't some natural disturbance. Men were talking, and he and Evangeline were almost able to understand what they said.

"Tommyknockers try to warn miners of cave-ins or damp."

"Or flooding?" Slocum said sarcastically.

"Yes, that, too. I've known several miners who heard their warnings."

"And were saved by them?"

"Yes, and Thompson was one of them. He told me he worked in a lead mine years back and heard a voice whisper in his ear 'timber' and he checked. The support timbers were rotted through. The mine would have been his grave if he hadn't heeded the warning."

"Tommyknockers," Slocum grumbled. But he tried to home in on the voices. They faded again, and then a new sound came that he easily recognized. Somebody drilled into rock so hard that the vibration made Slocum think he was the one swinging the heavy sledgehammer.

"The voices," Evangeline said, crowding close behind him. "They've gone away. Drowned out by that sound."

"Miners banging holes in a rock wall," Slocum said. "About here." He pressed his hands against the wall and felt every blow all the way up to his shoulders. "They'll be through in a minute or two."

"Then we're saved?"

"Looks like," Slocum said. Then he stepped back and stared at the wall

"What's wrong, John?"

"They've stopped drilling."

"They might be taking a break," Evangeline said.

"Run," Slocum said, realizing what was happening on the far side of the wall. "Run like hell!"

His arms circled her and herded her back the way they had come. In his rush he dropped his candle. It snuffed itself out on the floor. And Evangeline's fell from her hand. It burned on, having landed so the candle lay on its side. But there wasn't time to pick it up.

"Wh—?"

Slocum grunted as he scooped her up and stumbled fast into the tunnel. He didn't have time to explain. But she was struggling, fighting him in an effort to be put back down. When Evangeline pushed hard at him, Slocum fell to his knees. Then a huge hand pushed him and Evangeline along the drift. He lay atop her as they skidded. Her screams told him how her skin was being peeled away by the rough rock. And then her screams disappeared entirely.

Slocum lay atop her, deafened and blind. Every breath sucked in a lungful of dust. A shower of pebbles from the roof left Slocum and Evangeline covered like a newly closed grave.

He felt the woman stir beneath him, then begin to kick and shove. He arched his back and got some of the debris off, but it wasn't fast enough for her.

"What do you think you're doing? What just happened?" She put her hands on his shoulders and pushed hard, getting out from under him. He collapsed with the weight of the rock atop him.

"Oh my God," she exclaimed. "The mine collapsed!" She began digging furiously to get him free. By the time the last rock was removed and Slocum sat up, the ringing in his ears had died down. He still spoke too loudly.

"Blast," he shouted. "The miners were drilling holes to blast through rock. They didn't know there was already a tunnel on this side and used too much powder."

"We need to tell them. We have to get out. The whole mine might come down on us."

Slocum agreed but found it harder to stand than before. He felt a dozen cuts and scratches on his back where sharp stones had slashed him. But his hearing returned faster now and he heard Evangeline's footfalls going back toward the hole in the tunnel wall. She was shouting for help when a miner stuck his head through.

Slocum saw the man's face in the bright blue-white carbide light from his lamp. Who was more startled was a toss-up.

"Help us," Evangeline said, grabbing the miner and almost pulling him through the hole. "You've got to help us. We're trapped here."

"Whoa, little lady. Rein on back, now," the miner said. He disappeared through the hole but poked his head back in a few seconds later. "I told the foreman. He's on his way to see what's goin' on."

Slocum saw Evangeline kiss the man. Her lip prints remained on his cheek, where he was dirtiest.

"Well now, little lady, lemme help you."

Slocum stumbled along and said, probably too loudly, although his hearing was back, "You better take a close look at the blast. You cut into another mine. The whole damned thing might come tumbling down if you used too much powder."

"There's a passel of folks in there, ain't there?" the miner asked. He backed off again and several sets of hands began moving the rock from the hole until it was large enough for Evangeline to crowd through. Slocum followed immediately after her. The air on the new side of the wall wasn't any better, but it carried the smell of freedom to him. There was an elevator that went to the surface and a wide-open sky stretching overhead. He had nothing against working in a mine but preferred the sun and stars and the wind blowing in his face.

"What mine's this?" Slocum asked.

"You don't know?" The miner scratched his chin and stared hard at Slocum. "This here's the Molly Magee, the richest goldarn mine in Teller County."

"Got to agree," Slocum said. "There's no price that can be put on getting the hell out from being trapped underground."

"How'd you get in that other mine?" The man thrust his head back in and looked around. "No gold to be had there, is there? Means this vein done petered out on us. Or them varmints what dug the other tunnels already stole away the gold some time back."

"You came in from the west side of the mountain, didn't you?"

"Yep."

"They came in from the east. Whatever mine it is was abandoned years back."

"Might be the Shakespeare. Guy named Lear bought it from a couple of down-and-out prospectors. Didn't know we was so close, though. Lear was a laughingstock for buyin' such a worthless hole in the ground."

"Where'd they come from?" A harsh voice cut through the chatter of the miners already gathered at the end of the drift. Slocum saw a burly man, shoulders scraping the sides of the tunnel, pushing his way forward. "And why the hell ain't ya all workin'?"

"No cause to, Mr. Jensen," said the miner who'd spoken to Slocum. "We blasted right on through to the Shakespeare. No reason to keep workin'. We'd do a sight better gettin' up a level and followin' the new drift."

"The hell you say?" Jensen thrust his head through the hole, then drew back, eyeing Slocum briefly and Evangeline a lot longer. Her dress had been torn all up and down the front, leaving delectable sections of white skin open to any leering miner's gaze. She was unaware that her slide along the mine floor had left her in such dishabille.

"All we want is to go to the surface," Evangeline said.

"Don't want no wimmen down here, that's for certain," the foreman said. "Bad luck." He paused a moment, unable to take his eyes off her. Slocum saw how his carbide light worked up and down slowly but came to rest on Evangeline's breasts, where one almost peeked out from her ripped blouse. "Don't I know you?"

"I am Morgan Haining's daughter, sir," Evangeline said.

"Yeah, right. I remember seein' you now."

"How'd you ever fergit sich a lovely lassie?" a miner mumbled.

"Well, this is the Molly Magee and you got a free ride to the surface. But how'd you end up in that mine?" The foreman sniffed again, wiped his nose on his sleeve, and began to look worried.

"It's a long story. We'll let you know on our way topside," Slocum said.

Then his nose started to water, too. In spite of the dust

and closed-in air he had endured in the Shakespeare, his nose hadn't watered like this.

"Why'd they shutter the other mine?" Slocum asked suddenly. "They just mine out all the ore?"

"That's what I heard," a miner piped up.

"Like hell. They hit gas. Kept killin' off entire shifts of miners," the foreman said. He wiped his nose again.

"Gas?" Evangeline looked uneasy at the thought. Slocum was getting more than uneasy.

"We have to get the hell out of here," he said. "You blasted open another pocket of gas."

"Damnation, *that's* makin' my nose run like a faucet!" Jensen swung around and bellowed at the top of his lungs. "All candles out. Get your white asses out of the tunnel pronto!"

The miners who had blasted through the wall dropped their tools and lit out like scalded dogs. The foreman wasn't far behind.

"We have to get out of here fast," Slocum said, taking Evangeline's arm and getting her moving. "The whole mine can explode at any second."

"Gas. Thompson used to talk about it. But I don't smell anything."

"You might not. But that's what's making your nose drip. Mine and Jensen's, too."

"Nose?" Evangeline reached up and found her nose leaking. "Why, how rude of me."

She turned and started to walk, then turned at a right angle and walked into the wall. She hit the rocky surface and recoiled, her knees buckling under her. Slocum knew she was breathing too much of the released methane and not getting enough good air. He was feeling woozy himself, but he couldn't leave her. Dropping to his knees, he went to her, grabbed an arm, and began dragging her along. In the far reaches of his mind he heard himself chuckling. First the blast had shredded the front of Evangeline's dress. And now he was pulling her along a different mine floor and tearing the other side.

It was funny. But he couldn't laugh. He kept moving along like some beast of burden, but the going got harder every instant. His head swung like the weight at the end of a Regulator clock pendulum. The last fleeting thought that darted through his mind was the irony of surviving being dumped into a pit and trapped in a played-out mine only to be gassed when rescue was a matter of seconds away.

Then he passed out, Evangeline already unconscious beneath him.

In one lunge, Joe managed to knock his own thumb against the cold metal of the gun. He did nothing more important than depress the decocking lever and lower the hammer slowly. The bullet didn't come shooting out his way as the owner of the gun pulled the trigger only to find the action didn't work.
The thunderous report was muffled slightly.
Joe reached up and grabbed. Bloody skin came away in his fist.

16

Slocum took a deep sniff and felt life surge through his body. He smiled. He knew that scent. Evangeline. Whatever perfume she used, he appreciated it, and it stirred him to action. He took another breath and found his nose all clogged. He shook his head and raised up a few inches and realized that he had passed out. His face had been pressed down into her ample bosom. What little remained of her dress had gone up Slocum's nostrils as he sucked in one shallow breath after another.

What would normally have suffocated him had saved his life instead. The cloth had filtered enough of the deadly gas to bring him back to consciousness. He wasted no time tightly fastening his filthy bandanna around his mouth and nose as a crude guard against inhaling more of the methane. Every time he sucked in more air he tasted blood and dirt. That gave him an added goad to begin moving again, dragging Evangeline under him. He wished he could tie her hands around his neck. That would let him keep both of his hands on the mine floor as he made his way slowly in the direction already taken by the miners.

He pulled her twenty yards, then had to rest. He readjusted his bandanna and looked for something to put over Evangeline's mouth. If she could recover enough to help him get her out, that would be a boon without price. But her dress was so tattered no strip remained that would be useful. More than that, Slocum felt the pressure of time bearing down on him. This much gas released meant an explosion was imminent. The flicker of a miner's candle or the hiss of calcium carbide in its water bath would set off a blast that would kill him and Evangeline outright.

Even if the blast didn't kill them, the sudden lack of oxygen from the rapid combustion would. Or the mine collapsing on top of them. Or a dozen other deadly problems. Slocum kept crawling, pulling Evangeline along. He did this for hours. Days. An eternity. Longer.

And then suddenly he floated upward. Light as a feather on a spring breeze, he was on his feet and sailing along.

"Git them outta here. How'd he manage to pull her that far?"

"No good idea 'bout that, Mr. Jensen," Slocum heard someone answer. "Then again, they survived us blowin' down a wall right in front of 'em."

"The hell with it. Get that elevator down here. We gotta reach the surface pronto," Jensen said.

"No," Slocum gasped out. "Don't, spark, the gas!"

"He's right, Mr. Jensen," a miner said uneasily. "The way that damn thing comes down is a crime. But it also sparks as its chains rattle and drag along the walls. That'd make it a deadly crime. 'Gainst us."

The foreman cursed under his breath for a moment.

As he considered what to do to get his crew out of the dangerous mine, Jensen began pacing. This gave Slocum the chance to pull Evangeline upright and lean her against a wall. His vision was blurred, and he had to force his face almost to hers before her fine features came into focus. Her nostrils flared slightly, telling him she was alive. He placed a hand on her almost-naked breast and felt the thready beat of her heart.

"She's in a bad way," Slocum said as loudly as he could. His voice was still a hoarse whisper, but the mine foreman heard.

"Should never let wimmen down into a mine," he grumbled.

"We didn't have much choice," Slocum said.

"Mr. Jensen," a miner said apprehensively. "I think we got damp risin' mighty fast. The bird's done up and died."

This set off another string of profanity from the foreman.

"We can't get the elevator cage down in time. That means we have to start up. Use the ladders, boys. Get on up to the next level and keep climbing."

"Ain't got enough ladders fer that," a miner said. "We need to pull up the one we jist climbed."

"Then pretend you're a damn monkey and get up there." Jensen turned to Slocum. "Can you get her up a level?"

"I'll get her all the way to the surface if you furnish the ladder," Slocum vowed.

Jensen looked at him, a mixture of awe and contempt in his eyes. He admired Slocum for such courage and thought he was a fool for not saving his own life all at once.

"I'll need her tied onto my back. You have some rope?"

"Use her dress," Jensen said. Then he saw that there wasn't much left. His eyes changed to appreciation and not a little lust. This faded quickly. He swung about, barked at his miners to get to climbing, then found enough rope for Slocum to bind Evangeline's wrists and drape her over his back, her hands pulling hard against his Adam's apple. He staggered under the added weight, eyed the ladder extending up into the darkness of the next higher level, and put his hands on the rungs.

"You want to go ahead of us?" Slocum asked the foreman. "I might slow you up." He knew he and Evangeline might get stranded for the good of the entire mining crew. He saw no reason for separating Jensen from his crew.

"Naw, you go on up. I kinda like the view from down here."

Slocum looked back, anger flaring. What few tatters remained on Evangeline's body barely covered her privates from anyone lower on the ladder. Then his ire subsided when he realized that the miners weren't as likely to pull up the ladder if their foreman was still below.

"Give me a boost if I need it," Slocum said.

"Count on that," the foreman said, grinning. A gold tooth shone in the dim light filtering down from above.

Slocum wasted no more time. He took a deep breath, then began climbing at a steady pace. He had hoped to be able to make it up without stopping, but his strength seeped from him with every rung. Carrying his own weight would have been a chore, but with Evangeline hanging limply around his neck, almost strangling him, every rung was harder than the last. He was almost ready to cash it all in when strong hands grabbed him and pulled him to the next level. It took Jensen only seconds to scramble up from behind and pull the ladder.

"The gas is heavier than what we're breathin' here," the foreman said, "but I want to get the hell out of the mine. The sooner I get them fans workin' to vent the gas, the sooner you wastrels can get back to work."

"Especially since the canary died," another miner said. "She was 'bout the purtiest singin' bird I ever heard."

"Her last song was tellin' us to hightail it," said a miner already climbing the ladder to the next level.

Slocum followed, Evangeline stirring occasionally to let him know she was still alive. After five levels, Jensen bellowed for the elevator to be lowered. Slocum hoped the foreman knew what he was doing. The gas was deadly to breathe but explosive if a spark found it. But before he knew it, he and Evangeline were sitting in the bright sunlight. His head spun. He had no idea how long they had been underground or where they were.

Squinting, he looked around the mouth of the Molly Magee and saw a crowd slowly forming.

"Gas!" Jensen waved them back. "Get them pumps workin'. I want to hear nothin' but gasps comin' from the mine."

Heavy pumps began working, slowly at first and then

with greater speed. A steam engine powered the big fans near the mouth of the mine. At first all Slocum caught was the fetid air he had come to accept as normal. Then he gagged and turned away.

"That's the damp!"

Slocum wrapped his arms around Evangeline and began moving her away from the mine shaft. When he had pulled her a dozen yards she began to fight him weakly.

"No, no," she muttered. "Go 'way."

"You're safe. We're out of the mine," Slocum said. He grabbed a tarp and tossed it over her to keep the gawking miners from burning holes in her flesh with their hot stares.

"You want we should git a doctor?"

"Go fetch one," Slocum said. "I don't think she's too badly hurt. Just scratches. But some iodine and bandages will be in order. And water. Both of us." His raspy voice was loud enough to get the miners moving.

Jensen came over, turned an empty powder keg on end, and wiped at the grit on his face.

"You're 'bout the luckiest son of a bitch I ever did see," the foreman said. "What's happened to you and the lady there oughta killed you half a dozen times over."

"Tell me," Slocum said. "What's on the other side of this mountain?"

"Played out mines," Jensen said. "Same as over at the Low Down. The boss owns the whole danged mountain the mine's on. The Molly Magee has rights to ever' damn thing under this hill, just like Haining's the owner of his mountain."

"The Low Down's not too far off, is it?"

"Couple miles." Jensen looked harder at Evangeline. Her eyelids fluttered and the water dribbling across her lips was reviving her. "That there's Haining's girl, ain't it?"

"Evangeline Haining," Slocum acknowledged.

"You and her . . ." Jensen let the words trail off.

"High-graders tried to kill us. I was slugged and dumped in the other mine. Don't rightly know what happened to Miss Haining."

"I was going out riding, but they kidnapped me," she

said, struggling to sit up. Slocum supported her and let her drink her fill until she choked. "That's terrible water. Foul tasting." She grabbed his wrist and pulled the canteen back to her lips for another deep draught. This time she didn't choke. Her strength came flooding back.

"What did happen? Reckon you might want to let the marshal know," Jensen said.

"I was kidnapped," Evangeline said. A flush came to her cheeks as anger revitalized her. "And I think I know who did it. They caught me from behind and put a bag over my head. One whispered to the other that they were supposed to kill me, but the one who'd grabbed me refused. Couldn't do it."

"Because he wasn't a killer?" asked Jensen.

"Because he's sweet on me," Evangeline said.

"Miles?"

Slocum was startled when she shook her head.

"Singer," she said. "I've seen the way he looks at me. His partner—"

"Herk?"

"He's the one who was going to kill me because he'd been told to, but Singer convinced him to just dump me all trussed up like a Christmas goose and let me die in the mine of starvation."

"You'd have died of thirst long 'fore that," Jensen said. Slocum silenced further observations on how close to death Evangeline had come with a sharp look.

"What about you? You with the lady when this happened?" Jensen looked from Evangeline to Slocum and back, trying to make sense out of why the pair of them were together in the mine.

"I'm sure it was Miles who slugged me. Both Herk and Singer were up in the mine, getting the ore out they'd high-graded. The three of them have a sweet deal going, and they were close to being found out."

Slocum added it all up in his head as he sipped at the water a miner brought them. The Low Down foreman found where the veins of highest grade ore dived and dipped through the mountain, then had Herk and Singer enter from the far side and dig up into the veins while he ordered Haining's miners to work other stopes. That explained why the veins petered out fast. The high-graders had already stolen most of the ore by the time work started again in the Low Down.

But the real audacity came from loading the ore from the mine into their own wagon and taking it to the mill for smelting. Lucas Miles signed off on the bill, letting Haining pay for having his own gold stolen. Some gold—enough to keep the Low Down operational—returned to Morgan Haining to pay the bills. Or a few of them. The rest of the gold was hidden away somewhere so only Miles and his henchmen could haul it out later when they were ready to move on.

"You look strange, John," Evangeline said.

"Just reckoning how much of a score I have to even up. It's a big one, but something's not quite right."

"What are you saying? You don't believe Miles and Singer and Herk are responsible?"

"Oh, they're guilty as sin," Slocum said. "But I have to wonder if . . ." His voice trailed off.

"You're wondering why Papa isn't more involved in running the mine?"

"It's hard to miss the bills from the smelter. And unless I miss my guess, Miles has been charging other things to the Low Down that never arrived." Slocum remembered the spare axle he had seen Singer and Herk carrying in Cripple Creek.

"Papa is always worried," Evangeline said. "Too much so about the others."

"The others?" asked Jensen.

"Miners who have been injured. He supports quite a few men who were injured in the Low Down and cannot work any longer."

"What do you mean? He gives them money to live on? And they don't do work for it? Now that's the life," the

Molly Magee foreman said, shaking his head in disbelief. Slocum had to agree but said nothing. Morgan Haining's charity was his own business.

"Papa feels responsible. He considers it his Christian duty to provide charity for them."

Slocum wondered how much of the gold that Miles actually delivered went for such altruism. He had never heard of another mine owner spending one bent penny on workers injured while in their mines. It was nothing short of a miracle that the Low Down still operated, even with huge veins of gold so thick he could scrape it off with his fingernail.

"That's not the way to get rich," Jensen said.

"Papa doesn't want to get rich. He wants to do good with the gold."

"That's plumb crazy," the foreman said. Then he took a gander at the miners in a circle around them, all waiting to get a better look at the naked woman pulled from their mine shaft. "You folks gonna be here much longer? We got a crowd gatherin' and I want to get the men back into the mine. Looks like that pocket of gas is all pumped out."

"We have to get back to the Low Down," Slocum said. He thrust out his hand. For a moment Jensen hesitated, then grinned, the sunlight glinting off his gold tooth. They shook hands.

Then the foreman was off bellowing to his miners, chastising them for being so lazy and lollygagging in the middle of a shift.

"It's quite a walk back to the Low Down," Slocum said. "Are you up to it?"

"Of course I am," Evangeline said. "I will not have Miles working for Papa one instant longer. Or Herk and Singer."

"Even though Singer's sweet on you?" Slocum tried to josh her, but she wasn't having any of it. Evangeline stood, letting the tarp slip off her shoulders. This drew considerable attention from the miners waiting to take the elevator back into the bowels of the mountain. Slocum moved to block their view and hefted the canvas back around the woman's shoulders. Evangeline was so mad she shook.

"I didn't mean anything by it," he said.

"Oh, John, I'm so mad I could chew nails and spit tacks. Papa will *have* to fire them!"

Slocum said nothing. He wanted to do more than see the trio fired. If his Colt Navy wasn't still wrapped up in his gear, he would have insisted that Evangeline remain at the Molly Magee and he would see to a bit of six-gun justice immediately.

"Should we get Marshal Young? What they did was illegal. They can't kidnap me!"

Slocum aimed Evangeline in the direction of the road leading to the Low Down Mine and ignored her continuous ranting until they reached the bunkhouse. He started to fetch his six-shooter, but she grabbed his arm. With her bright blue eyes wide and imploring, she said, "No, not that, John. I don't want anyone killed."

"Even after what they did to you? I'm not as forgiving. If I hadn't had more than a touch of luck, I'd be dead at the bottom of a pit. And you would have died of thirst all tied up."

"I . . . I know. Let's talk with Papa first."

"You go find him."

"You won't shoot Miles or the others in the back, will you?"

"No," Slocum said. Mentally he added, *I want to see the fear in their eyes when I gun them down.*

"I'm sorry. That came out so awful. You would never shoot a man in the back. You're not like that."

"Go on. You might want to get some clothes before you hike on up to the office."

"I might find Papa at home. That's a good idea, John." She hesitated, then let the tarp slip a bit and moved close enough to give him a quick kiss as she brushed her nearly bare breasts against him. Evangeline gave him a wicked smile, spun, and hurried off. Slocum watched her go, wondering if he was making a mistake by not accompanying her. If Miles or his partners saw Evangeline, they'd know the cat was out of the bag. Killing her would be a quick way of keeping their high-grading going a little longer.

The best way he could guard the dark-haired beauty was to stop Lucas Miles. Permanently. He hurried into the deserted bunkhouse. All the miners were far underground working to pull low-grade ore from the mine while Herk and Singer worked the real mother lode.

Slocum rummaged through his bedroll and found his six-gun securely tucked away in its holster. He drew it out, spun the cylinder to be certain all six chambers were loaded, then pulled the gun belt tight around his waist and settled the ebony-handled six-shooter where it usually rode on his left hip.

"What're you doing—"

Slocum swung about. Standing in the bunkhouse doorway and outlined by the bright sunshine was the very man he wanted.

"Don't move, Miles," Slocum said. His hand was moving for his six-shooter even as he spoke.

17

Slocum cleared leather and got off a shot, but it went wide. Splinters from the door frame blasted outward, causing Lucas Miles to flinch away. Before Slocum could fan off another round, Miles stumbled backward and pulled the door shut. The second bullet ripped through the flimsy door panel. Cursing, Slocum ran to the door and yanked it open, ready to use a third round and make this one bury itself in Miles's vile heart.

The door slammed hard against the wall as Slocum flung it wide, but Miles had vanished like a ghost.

"Where are you, you lily-livered son of a bitch?" Slocum swung around to the left, then whirled right when he failed to spot Miles. He took three quick steps forward, knowing Miles had ducked around the side of the bunkhouse. But which way?

Slocum tried to remember the man's outline in the doorway. Had Miles been wearing a hogleg of his own? He hadn't gotten a good enough look to know for sure. And as angry as he was, it didn't matter. Let Miles fill him with lead. He had gotten out of the pit and the mine and sucked down gas and climbed up a mile of ladders with Evangeline on his back. What were a couple bullets?

His hot anger faded as he neared the edge of the bunkhouse, and a cold fury replaced it. Slocum knelt, chanced a quick look around, and was glad he had become more cautious. Miles fired and missed because he expected Slocum to come around the corner standing up. Slocum fired twice more at the foreman, then slipped back to let a bullet sing past.

He needed to reload, but the remaining two rounds would have to do.

"Let's do this like men, Miles," he called. "You and me, face to face. We draw and fire."

Slocum had no intention of giving the foreman the chance to ever get another shot at him. If Miles showed his face, Slocum would put a bullet smack in the middle of it. Rather than wait for an answer, Slocum ran past the front of the bunkhouse and around the other side, wary that Miles might try the same thing. Miles had more practice sneaking up behind men. To forget this would spell his own death. Slocum wasn't going to stop until he had put Miles into the ground.

He got to the far side of the bunkhouse, hurried to the rear, and chanced a peek around.

Miles was nowhere to be seen.

Had he decided to make a flat-out frontal attack on where Slocum had been? That didn't set well with what he knew of the foreman. Miles wasn't the sort of brave man to launch such an assault. Drawing back, Slocum carefully studied the land behind the bunkhouse. It sloped downhill fast and disappeared into a rocky ravine that carried spring runoff from the higher elevations. That had to be where Miles had gone.

The man was running for his life and had no intention of shooting it out.

Slocum slid down the hillside and dug in his heels a few feet from the edge. Stones tumbled into the ravine, giving him away. He flopped on his belly and cautiously peered over the edge into the now-dry ravine. If Miles had come this way, Slocum couldn't see him. There was no way that Slocum could track from up here—or maybe even in the ravine. The rock wasn't likely to take much of a track. For several minutes he lay still, listening harder than he looked.

Finally stirring, he thought he heard faint sounds from farther down the ravine. Miles might have gone in the other direction, but Slocum had a fifty-fifty chance of being right. And there was that faint scraping sound. While it might come from anything or anyone, Slocum was willing to bet that Miles was trying not to be heard as he made his way to what seemed like safety for him.

"The stables," Slocum muttered when he tried to get the lay of the land. He looked down into the ravine, then decided against jumping down and following Miles. The fist-sized stones littering the bottom would only turn his ankle. And around those larger rocks was a sea of pea-sized gravel. The going would be rough.

He scrambled back up the slope until he found a path leading to the outhouse behind the bunkhouse. From there he went directly to the stables. Slocum was panting harshly from his quick sprint. He lifted his six-shooter and aimed when he saw Miles bent low over the neck of a horse. Slocum's hand shook a mite, but he was steady enough for a good shot.

The problem was that Miles had already ridden out of range.

He hurried into the stables. Miles was on his own saddle horse. All that remained were the two nags used to pull the ore wagon. Knowing he had no choice, Slocum found a saddle and bridle and worked to put them on the stronger of the horses. For his effort he had to avoid a hoof lifted and trying to kick him. The horse didn't want to be ridden; it pulled loads and was too good to be carrying a rider.

Slocum prevailed. He swung into the saddle and channeled the horse's ire into speed.

"Hey, Slocum, where ya goin'?" called a miner.

"Got to get me a sidewinder," Slocum shouted back.

The answer was lost in the *clop-clop* of his horse's

hooves on rock. Slocum saw the Haining house set off to the side of the road and wondered if Evangeline had found her pa there. Probably not. Without allowing the horse to slow, Slocum glanced up the steep hill toward the solitary office perched on the crest. That was more likely where Morgan Haining spent his days. From what Evangeline said, he worried more about giving away his wealth than making it.

That level of charity made no sense to Slocum, and somehow he knew it was at the heart of the woes besetting the Low Down Mine. He turned back to the chase. From horseback he couldn't see fresh hoofprints in the dust. Too many other horses and wagons had rolled along here for a single set to be prominent, but Slocum doubted Miles was going to leave the road. The way he galloped along, he wanted to put as many miles between him and the mine as possible.

Lucas Miles, Herk, and Singer. It made sense they were all high-grading the ore from the Low Down. But Slocum still had the gut feeling he missed something. He was pretty sure it had been Miles who slugged him, and Evangeline was certain that Singer and Herk had kidnapped her and left her to die in the abandoned mine. All that was undeniable, but something was missing and it gnawed at Slocum like a dog on a bone.

The draft horse wouldn't go fast, but it kept up a steady pace that soon convinced Slocum he could overtake Miles. The foreman had pressed his horse and was exhausting it from galloping too long. If he had wanted to put the most distance between them he ought to have galloped, walked, trotted—changed the gait to rest the horse and let it prepare for the next all-out run. But he hadn't.

When Slocum topped a hill in the road, he saw Miles ahead, leading his horse. The animal limped a mite, giving Slocum hope that the horse had either thrown a shoe or had pulled up lame. Either way, Lucas Miles was his for the taking.

Slocum slowed and finally drew rein. His horse snorted loudly, shook its head, and took the occasion to relieve itself. Letting the horse do as it pleased for a moment, Slocum studied the countryside. Juniper and scrub oak grew to one side of the road. Some distance on the other side rose a stand of pine trees, too far for Miles to reach easily.

Leaving the road, Slocum circled and came up behind the grove of juniper. From the other side of the curtain of vegetation came the sound of a man cursing a blue streak. A slow smile came to Slocum's lips. He was close to his goal. Then the smile faded when he remembered he had not reloaded his Colt. At the very least he should have returned to the bunkhouse and gotten a spare loaded cylinder from his saddlebags.

"Two rounds," he muttered. "Ought to be enough."

He was going to confront a man who had tried to kill him more than once, with only two rounds in his six-shooter. He wished there had been a rifle with the saddle he had taken from the stables, but there was nothing under his right leg save for leather worn smooth from long, hard use.

Kicking his leg up and over, Slocum dismounted. The horse immediately tried to bolt, but he held it down. The reins slipped a bit in his hands, but he made certain the horse didn't get away. He knew he ought to let the horse graze but wasn't going to take off the bridle. The horse would gallop off for sure if he did that. Fastening the reins around a sturdy oak limb, Slocum made his way through the thicket toward the sounds of Miles struggling with his horse.

The last few yards were more difficult going because of the tangled blackberry thorns cutting at Slocum's legs. He crouched down when he was close enough to peer into the small clearing. Not ten feet away stood Miles's horse, but of its rider there was no sign. Slocum waited patiently, although the horse began pawing at the ground and giving signs that it had caught Slocum's scent.

Or was it Slocum that it reacted to?

Slocum threw himself sideways and avoided a bullet in the back. The slug ripped through the bushes in front of him and then kicked up a tiny cloud of dirt. A second bullet followed, but it was no better aimed than the first.

Swinging his six-gun around, Slocum was aware that he couldn't fire willy-nilly, not with only two rounds. He vainly hunted for Miles. The man had slunk back into the thicket, and from the sound of receding footsteps, he was running away.

Getting to his feet, Slocum went to the horse rather than after the foreman. He checked the horse's left rear leg and saw a gash just above the hock going several inches across the fetlock. Given attention, the cut would heal, but Miles wouldn't be able to return and gallop off on this horse. Slocum rummaged through the saddlebags and then moved to the right side of the horse. A grin crossed his lips.

He drew the Winchester from its saddle sheath and cocked it. The sound of a round chambering made his smile even broader. He shoved his six-gun back into its holster and knew he had a better chance now to bring down Miles. If he caught sight of him anywhere within a hundred yards, he would be dead within seconds. Slocum had spent the war as a sniper and had seldom missed his target. Although Lucas Miles didn't sport the bright gold braid of a Yankee officer, he was broad enough of shoulder to afford a decent bull's-eye.

Slocum itched to be after Miles, but caution sent him on a quick circuit of the clearing. He wasn't sure what he hunted but didn't want Miles circling and coming up on him from behind again. The foreman had already shown he was a better backshooter than he was a marksman.

Only when he was satisfied that Miles hadn't already returned did Slocum head into the woods. The blackberry bushes gave way to other thorny impediments, but when he found a game trail, he walked with lengthened stride until he found a boot heel print. Fresh.

Slocum slowed his advance and kept an eye peeled for any movement in the woods. When he found a bit of Miles's shirt caught on a thorn he knew the man wasn't sticking around. He was hightailing it for the high country and leaving his limping horse behind.

The grove gradually petered out and a long open stretch led up into the foothills. Grass in the meadow clearly showed where Miles had gone. From the distance between the footprints, Miles was running as fast as he could. Slocum followed at a more leisurely pace. Miles had worn out his horse. He hadn't learned. He would wear himself out as well.

The meadow gave way to another stand of trees, but these were sparser, and in less than twenty minutes Slocum saw Miles ahead. As he had expected, Miles had run himself to ground. From the way he dragged his leg, he must have turned his ankle. Knowing this could be a trap, Slocum carefully studied the ground Miles had already crossed. He spotted the tumble of rocks that had brought the foreman up lame.

Slocum lifted his borrowed rifle, considered the irony of using Miles's own rifle, then squeezed off a shot. Miles threw up his hands and fell forward, screaming until he hit the ground. It hadn't been a killing shot. Slocum had enough experience to know he had only winged Miles, but the foreman wasn't going to be doing any running—or limping.

"Slocum, hold on. You got me. Don't kill me!"

"Where'd I hit you? Felt like I hit you in the thigh. Left or right?"

"Left. My ankle was already startin' to swell like a rattlesnake-struck dog. I ain't goin' nowhere. I surrender."

Slocum doubted it. The man had just tried to shoot him in the back.

Approaching slowly, a fresh cartridge under the rifle hammer, Slocum saw Miles give a single twitch and then lay still. He might have hit something real important. A man could bleed to death in less than a minute if the bullet nicked the femoral artery. But Slocum didn't see that kind of blood pooling around Miles.

His caution paid off—and Miles's impatience did him in. Before Slocum had gotten closer than twenty feet, Miles rolled over and opened fire. The last bullet stung Slocum's left hand and tore the rifle from his grip. Fingers bleeding and rifle ruined, he drew his six-shooter. Two rounds remained.

He used the first one to hit Miles in the right shoulder.

"You're not going anywhere," Slocum said. "Except to the cemetery." He cocked his Colt Navy and aimed.

"No, no, I give up. You can't kill a man who's surrendered." Miles clumsily tossed away his six-gun. It landed with a dull thud some distance away. Even if Slocum hadn't shot him in the leg and shoulder, he couldn't have reached it.

Slocum walked to Miles, still wary.

"Why are you tryin' to kill me?" the foreman asked.

"That's about the damnedest, stupidest thing I ever heard," Slocum said. If Miles was playing for time, this was hardly the way to do it. Reminding a man of the attempts on his life wasn't going to save your own when you stared down the muzzle of a six-shooter.

But Slocum didn't pull the trigger. He stared at Miles. The man was scared shitless. That was obvious. But he didn't look as if he understood why Slocum was gunning for him, either.

"Look, Slocum, I don't like you. Truth is, I hate your guts, but why kill me?"

"You dumped me in the pit to die, that's why."

"What pit?"

Slocum came closer to believing the man, but not quite.

"You slugged me when I was driving the ore wagon back from the mill. I didn't get a real good look but I'm pretty sure it was you."

"Of course it was me. I buffaloed you 'cuz you was sniffin' around where you weren't welcome."

"I figured out how you were high-grading and stealing the gold. And how you were making Haining pay for smelting the ore you stole from him."

"I don't know what yer talkin' 'bout."

Again Slocum almost believed him. Miles was too frightened to lie this convincingly.

"You aren't stealing from Haining? I saw Herk and Singer moving ore out of the mine shaft that undercuts the Low Down."

"Them? I wouldn't put nuthin' past that pair. Mr. Haining told me to keep an eye on them but I never caught 'em doin' nuthin'. I was always too busy with . . ."

Miles's words trailed off. Slocum's mind had begun turning over what the foreman was telling him and had been lulled into believing the wounded man wasn't dangerous. His six-shooter came up and he fired his last round just as Miles managed to pull a derringer free from his pants pocket.

Miles's shot went wide. Slocum's hit the foreman smack between the eyes.

"You poor bastard," Slocum said. The pieces were all falling together in a way that meant a world of woe. He turned and left, nursing his wounded left hand. It was going to be a long ride back to the Low Down and what he had to do there.

18

It was past sundown by the time Slocum got back to the Low Down Mine. His horse hadn't minded the slow walk since Slocum had been on foot but had occasionally balked because Slocum was leading the horse Miles had ridden. The cut on the rear leg had to hurt the saddle horse something fierce, but Slocum wasn't about to abandon a good mount. Some liniment, a bandage, and a week of oats and rest would put the horse back into riding condition again. Slocum saw no reason why the horse didn't belong to him now, in way of payment for all Miles had done to him.

Whether to leave Miles's body for the buzzards and coyotes had been a harder decision. Slocum had finally slung the body over the ore wagon horse's back and had walked himself, knowing Miles's horse could never handle weight beyond the saddle on it. He was almost as footsore as Miles's horse, but he had done the right thing. Bury the son of a bitch out in the potter's field. He didn't deserve more. But from what Slocum had figured out, he didn't deserve much less, either.

"Glory be, Slocum," the stable hand said, eyes wide when he saw the mine foreman draped over the horse. "What happened? Did Miles run into them road agents?"

"He ran afoul of me," Slocum said simply. The stable

hand swallowed hard and looked like he wanted to be somewhere else—anywhere else—rather than spend another second with a killer. "You take real good care of his horse. I don't know how that fetlock got cut, but the cannon bone's in good shape. The pastern's not damaged, either."

"Nope, just a deep gash. I kin fix it up." The stable hand looked up and started to say more but thought better of it.

"Do that." Slocum unsaddled the ore wagon horse and patted its neck. While not the usual ride he was accustomed to, the horse had done all he had asked of it. Now it could go back to pulling heavy loads of gold ore down to the mill.

"Uh, Slocum, whatcha gonna do with Miles? Or what's left of him?" The man's curiosity had finally tipped the scales back into talking to a man he knew to be a stone killer.

"I ought to take him up to the office. Is Haining there?"

"Don't rightly know. What'd the boss want with a corpse? It's already startin' to smell."

"Miles never did anything else," Slocum said. He unlashed the cords he had used to fasten Miles's wrists and ankles, bent and heaved, getting the dead man over his shoulder. After the long miles he had walked, Slocum was a mite wobbly, but he got his feet under him and left the stables. He heard the stable hand muttering to himself as he began tending the horse's leg.

Slocum looked around, then turned for the mine headquarters and hiked uphill. He was winded by the time he reached Haining's office. With a quick twist, he dumped the body down against the wall and went inside. Nobody was going to steal a corpse.

Morgan Haining looked up, startled.

"I didn't hear you, Slocum. What can I do for you? I'm very busy."

"Got Miles outside."

"Well, tell him to get inside. I need to give him some orders. New drift opened. Randolph thinks he has found another new vein of considerable assay. That's two in a week, the one you uncovered and a new one." Haining's eyes glowed, but it came from tiredness, not excitement at the gold he would pull from his mine.

"Miles isn't in any condition to talk right now."

"Drunk? I warned him. I warned him. If he's drunk, tell him he's fired. I can't abide by such behavior. It's a bad example for the men, and with Evangeline spending so much time around the mine, I can't take any chances."

Slocum considered his options. He could tell Haining straight out that Miles was dead, but another idea came to him.

"I'll let him know. I don't think he'll put up much of a fuss over it."

"Good," Haining said decisively. Then, with a touch of doubt in his voice, he asked, "Can I ask a favor of you, Slocum?"

Slocum waited.

"I need someone trustworthy to take, uh, envelopes into town."

"To the bunkhouse you own and let the injured miners use?"

Haining looked at him sharply. "I had asked Evangeline about you, and she seemed impressed. I have been struck by your diligence and integrity, also. Yes, I help those unfortunates who were injured in my mine."

From the way Haining ran his fingers over the fat envelope on the desk in front of him, Slocum guessed it was harder and harder for the mine owner to fulfill what he thought were his charitable obligations.

"When do you want me to deliver the money?"

"I, uh, in a few days. I need you to drive another couple of loads of ore to the mill first thing tomorrow morning, if you're able. From the look of your arm, it's healing, but you do seem to be under the weather. Will you be able to do this small chore for me?" The mine owner chewed on his lower lip and looked away.

Slocum nodded and left when it became obvious Haining had run out of words. Closing the door behind him, Slocum looked down at Miles's body and knew he had to move the foreman before he rotted any more. The time wasn't right for Haining to know what had happened. The stable hand would undoubtedly spread the word among the miners, but Haining had little contact with them.

Grunting, Slocum hefted the body and went back down the hill, sorry now he hadn't left Miles for the coyotes. It wouldn't have been too hard to simply keep on riding, but he still had a score to settle. If not on his own account, then for Evangeline. Herk and Singer had kidnapped her. They were likely to do something desperate when she popped up again.

Miles had a small shack some distance from the main bunkhouse. Slocum kicked open the door and dropped the body onto the cot. He stepped back and looked around, hoping to find some evidence of where Miles had hidden the gold he had stolen from the Low Down. After fifteen minutes of poking into corners, Slocum gave up the hunt. Miles and his cronies had undoubtedly stashed the gold and had no reason to make a map. If he looked hard enough around the mine where they had burrowed under the Low Down's mother lode, he would probably find more than a few gold bars.

He closed the door behind him and looked to the office where Haining still toiled to find another few dollars to support his injured miners, and then to the man's house. Lights blazed in the front window. Slocum wanted to talk with Evangeline again but knew it wasn't a good idea at the moment. He changed his mind when he saw two dark forms approach the house's porch and vault over the railing rather than go up the front steps.

Slocum hurried to the house, his hand rubbing the cold ebony butt of his six-shooter. Again he had misjudged. He carried an empty six-shooter when he might need a fully loaded one.

He neared the house, then crouched down and duck-walked until he was under the parlor window where he could eavesdrop. Slocum's hand gripped his six-shooter even tighter when he heard what was being said inside.

"You're utter fools, both of you!" Darleen Haining's anger snapped like a blacksnake whip. "You can't do the simplest chore!"

"Aw, Darleen, it ain't like that," Singer said. "Not at all."

"She's alive. She's alive! You were supposed to get rid of her, and she waltzes back into the house as if nothing had happened."

"We, I mean, Singer, he got cold feet," Herk said. "Wasn't my fault. It was all his. He's sweet on her and couldn't kill her like you wanted. I was going to kill her like you wanted, but he couldn't do it."

"You both make me sick." Darleen crossed her arms and glared at her henchmen.

"Don't make you sick when we bring all that gold outta the mine," said Singer. "Don't make you sick when we take those invoices you do up and collect twice from your husband fer supplies. Don't make you sick when—"

"I didn't say you were useless," Darleen interrupted, her voice softening. Slocum rose and chanced a quick look inside the parlor. Morgan Haining's wife reached out and lightly caressed Singer's cheek. Then her arm tensed and she raked her fingernails along the cheek she had just stroked so lovingly.

"Ow, that hurts!"

"Maybe you'll remember how much it hurts when you disobey me."

"You want we should get rid of her now?" Herk looked eager to please. If Singer lusted after Evangeline, it was clear that Herk had his sights set on her mother. From the way Darleen cozied up to him, Herk might well have been getting his lust sated as a way of keeping him in line.

"No, you idiot," Darleen snarled. "I have to find out how she got away. What did you do with her, anyway?

You certainly didn't kill her and hide the body like I wanted."

"We—Singer—tied her up and we left her in the old mine. There's no way she coulda got free. We tied her up real good. And she'd never find her way out of the mine. We lowered her, made sure she was all trussed up and tied to an ore cart, and then we pulled the rope back up the shaft. There's no elevator or nuthin'."

"You didn't even dump her down the mine shaft," Darleen said, marveling at how foolish her henchmen were.

"Well, no, Singer thought . . ."

"Singer never had a thought in his life. Neither have you," Darleen said savagely. "I'll find out how she got away and if she has any clue that you two were responsible."

"No, she couldn't," Singer said fast. His voice was pitched too high, telling Slocum that he lied. Darleen heard the lie, also.

"Good," she said. "You've done that much right. What about Miles?"

"Ain't seen him all day."

"I haven't see him, either. I ought to . . . talk with him."

"Why?" Herk asked. "He don't mean shit to you."

"No, he doesn't, my darling," Darleen said. Herk cringed when the woman stroked over his stubbled cheek. He expected the same raking nails that his partner had got. She took pleasure in the fact that she controlled him so easily. "He's never meant anything to me, but he's useful. Dear Lucas never once questions the extra loads of ore you furnish because I ask him ever so nicely."

Slocum turned and pressed his back against the wall of the house. Miles had been a bigger fool than he had thought. The foreman wasn't collecting the gold from the mine—he was taking out his payment from what Darleen had obviously offered freely in exchange for looking the other way and ignoring the blatant high-grading.

"He might be taking Slocum far, far away."

"You think so, Darleen?" asked Herk. "It was kinda surprisin' when we saw Miles slug Slocum like he did."

"I told him to. There was no way Slocum would not find out about how the mill was being billed for all the smelted ore. He had a nasty habit of asking too many questions."

"We coulda got rid of him," Singer said.

"You tried, you failed. As you have too many times. I got tired of waiting, so I asked Miles to do what he could for me."

Slocum had his six-gun halfway out of his holster before he remembered he was carrying an empty cylinder. All his brushes with death down in the mine had been caused by these three, not Lucas Miles. Except that last plunge down into the pit. That had been Miles's doing, and the lying son of a bitch had died for it.

Like Herk and Singer would die. Slocum wasn't the least bit inclined to turn them over to Marshal Young, if the man would even concern himself with anything that happened outside town. But what should he do with Darleen? The woman had as much as admitted she had ordered her own daughter's death. Slocum couldn't believe any mother would so coldly do that.

And for what? Her motives made no sense.

Slocum wasn't in much of a mood to figure it all out. Why Darleen Haining did what she did wasn't important. She had ordered her own daughter killed. Lucas Miles had been sent on a similar mission to get rid of Slocum since he was finding out too much about the high-grading.

Darleen had to know she couldn't keep stealing from the Low Down forever, but greed drove her to try for just a few more ounces of gold. Or was that bars of gold? With the vein Slocum had found and the new one unearthed by Randolph, it might be more than that. Although he had pushed away the notion of figuring out the woman's reasons, they still gnawed away at the edges of his mind. All she had to do was ask Morgan Haining. The man *owned* the mine.

Slocum went to the front of the house in time to see Herk and Singer hurrying away. They were swallowed by the darkness within seconds, leaving Slocum to stew in his own juices over what to do.

He glanced at the front door of the Haining house and knew Evangeline was on the other side. So was her mother, but from what Slocum had overheard, Evangeline was safe enough for the time being. Later, that might not be true, but for the moment she was safe. He returned to the bunkhouse, his mind working furiously on what he could do to even the score.

"You sure two'll be enough?" Randolph looked skeptically at the team Slocum had hitched to the ore wagon. "Not strong."

"They'll do me just fine," Slocum said, remembering to face Randolph so the man could read his lips. He glanced behind at the load of ore ready to be taken to the mill. To one side a tarpaulin had been thrown over the rest of his cargo.

"You be on watch," Randolph said. "More gold later." The giant of a man pointed to a huge hill of ore brought up from the mine by the eager miners. They all scented bonuses for their work, and Slocum didn't blame them. If anything, the new vein Randolph and his son had discovered looked as if it would assay out even higher than the other. There might be fifty or sixty ounces to the ton, and the miners were bringing up several tons a shift.

"I wish the freight wagon had been found," Slocum said. There hadn't been enough men hunting to retrieve the wagon or the supplies Slocum had lost earlier on his way back from Cripple Creek. Since then, he had been too preoccupied staying alive to track down the solitary road agent.

"Two much better," Randolph said. Then he waved for Slocum to get moving. Jawing wouldn't get the ore smelted.

Slocum got the two horses pulling. They weren't as strong as the ones he had used before, but they were up for the early morning task. Slocum's arms felt better, and he used both hands on the reins. Some weakness remained in his left arm, but anticipation kept him keyed up and feeling strong.

He maneuvered the wagon out onto the road and then down into the valley, where the mill was already in full operation. Humming to himself as he drove, he did as Randolph had bid. He kept an eye peeled for Herk and Singer. The men had failed at too many deadly tasks set by Darleen Haining. They would do everything possible not to fail again.

As he passed the old mine, Slocum had to look up at the mouth. He hoped to catch a glimpse of the men, possibly working to steal the ore out from under Haining's nose but more likely laying in wait to ambush him. The wagon clanked and rattled past the pile of newly mined high-graded ore and down the steeper slope into the valley without Slocum once spotting the men. He tugged with increasing strength on the reins and slowed the horses. The wagon rolled to a stop in front of the door leading to the crusher.

The mill foreman waved to Slocum.

"How long'll it take to unload this time?" Slocum asked.

"You in a big hurry to get back?"

"Got this much more to haul down," Slocum said. "If I don't bother with a noon meal, I can bring a third load."

"You're makin' me a damn fortune," the foreman joked. He waved to half a dozen men, who set to unloading the cargo. Slocum cast a quick glance at the tarp but said nothing, standing at the side of the wagon nearest it. He began working to untie the tarp.

He swung around when he heard someone coming up on him from behind.

"We got the drop on you, Slocum. Don't turn around," Herk said.

Slocum glanced over his shoulder. He had been careless. He had no idea where Singer and Herk had been hiding, but he had failed to see them.

"You going to shoot me in the back with all these witnesses?" Slocum pointed to the men moving the ore from the wagon.

"We don't want to kill you at all," Singer said, "but we got orders."

"You're both fools," Slocum said.

"You son of a bitch. You take that back," growled Herk.

"Don't get so riled," Singer advised his partner. "He wants to get us to thinkin' 'bout somethin' else, that's all he's doin'."

"Come on. We're gonna mosey over to the grinding wheels," Herk said.

"I got a proposition," Slocum said. "I've thought up a scheme to make a fortune high-grading the Low Down ore."

"Oh, yeah?" Herk laughed harshly. "Why should we listen to you?"

"I can make you rich. The scheme's foolproof. Nobody'd ever know what was going on. I can guarantee you each a hundred dollars a day." Such a princely sum would have provoked some reaction in an honest man. Both Herk and Singer laughed.

"What? You don't want to get rich?" demanded Slocum. "I tell you, I know how to—"

"We don't care to hear no scheme, Slocum," Singer said. "We're already makin' twice that a day. Each."

"You're high-grading the mine? You're stealing gold from Mr. Haining?"

"You ain't stupid, Slocum. You know we are."

"That's what I was afraid I'd hear," Morgan Haining said, rising up from under the tarp. He threw it back and leveled a sawed-off shotgun at the men. "You boys drop those six-shooters."

Singer let out a yelp and bolted. He got two paces before Slocum tackled him. As they wrestled, the shotgun blared and Herk screamed once before he died.

Knowing that his partner was suddenly buzzard bait took all the fight out of Singer. He sagged under Slocum's grip.

"Get up," Slocum said, grabbing Singer by the collar and pulling him to his feet. He swung him around to face Morgan Haining. Singer was shaking like a leaf.

"Mr. Haining, I didn't have any part of it," Singer stammered out.

"You are both a thief and a liar," Haining said, glaring at the miner. "I ought to—" He lifted his shotgun. The barrel still smoked from the discharge that had killed Herk.

"He was the one who was screwin' yer wife!" Singer blurted. "She was the one who thought up the scheme. She made us do it. I was greedy but *he* wanted her. And he got her!"

Haining's face went white. He opened his mouth and then snapped it shut. He stepped forward and swung the stock of the shotgun around and connected with the point of Singer's chin. The man collapsed without making a sound.

"He's right," Slocum said.

"What?"

"He's right about what he said. About your wife and Herk."

"You can't say a thing like that!" Anger flared in the mine owner's eyes, but his face lacked any hint of emotion. "You liar! Darleen would never consort with the likes of these men. Now *you're* telling lies about her!"

Haining swung his shotgun around and poked its rough-edged muzzle into Slocum's belly, causing Slocum to stumble back. Slocum saw the man's finger drawing back on the second trigger. There was no way he could draw and fire before Haining cut him in half. And there was no way he could run.

Haining's finger turned white as he applied pressure on the shotgun's trigger.

19

"You're a damned liar," Morgan Haining said. His face was a mask of anger and his hands shook. Slocum looked from the finger tensing on the shotgun trigger to the man's eyes. He saw more than anger there. He saw fear.

Fear that Slocum wasn't lying.

"We can talk about this. Put down the shotgun."

"Take it back." Haining's face was still a frozen mask, but his eyes turned into something that Slocum feared more. They were the eyes of a man who knew his world had come crashing down in ruin. They were the eyes of a man with nothing left to lose.

"She's a whore," Slocum said coldly. "Killing me won't change that. She got what she wanted from Miles. She got what she wanted from Herk."

"No, no, you're wrong! She's my wife!"

Slocum got ready to feint right and dive left, hoping that Haining wouldn't be alert enough to follow. He saw that his chance of living was next to nothing. Haining intended to murder him, as if that might erase the truth.

"Papa! Put that down! You don't want to kill him!" Evangeline Haining came from the smelter, pushing past the mill foreman and storming out to plant herself between Slocum and the shotgun.

"He's lying. They're all lying. I won't tolerate that. He can't call my darling Darleen a whore!"

"Put . . . it . . . down," Evangeline said. Every word was plain, distinct, and carried the same crack of command that Slocum had heard in her mother's voice when Darleen had talked to Herk and Singer.

Haining went to push her away, but she stepped forward and grabbed the sawed-off barrels and pulled them to her own belly.

"Shoot and be damned!" Evangeline raged. "You can't kill him. I won't let you."

"She's your mother." Haining sounded a little less sure of himself now. Slocum touched his six-shooter and then let his hand fall away. The shooting was over. Haining was giving up.

"She's my stepmother," Evangeline said. "She's never loved me. She's never *liked* me. At best, she tolerated me because of you. Now we know why she did. The gold."

"No, no."

Haining collapsed, falling to his knees. Slocum watched as Evangeline hugged her pa close. Carefully circling the two, Slocum reached out and snared the shotgun, pulling it out of the mine owner's hand. He tossed the shotgun into the rear of the wagon, and only then did he heave a sigh of relief. He stared at the pair, unmoving except for Haining's body-wracking sobs. Slocum hadn't realized Darleen was Evangeline's stepmother. Things that hadn't made complete sense before now fell into place.

His gaze locked with Evangeline's, her blue eyes filled with tears. Silent communication passed between them. Slocum had one more thing to do. He climbed into the empty ore wagon and looked down at the mill foreman.

"Keep the Low Down gold for a while. Mr. Haining will let you know when it's all right to send it back up to him." The foreman looked at Herk's body, cut almost in half, and nodded numbly. Slocum snapped the reins and began working the rig around to get back onto the road to the mine.

Slocum had left the wagon at the foot of the hill where the Low Down office stood, but he watched the Haining house like a hawk. He had seen movement inside the parlor—in the same parlor window where he had spied on Darleen Haining and overheard her involvement in the high-grading at the mine. He hitched up his gun belt and wondered if he could shoot down a woman.

Slocum knew he could, but he wanted to hear just a bit more from Darleen Haining before it came down to gunplay.

He went to the house, paused at the steps, and looked around. The day was about perfect. Summer in the Colorado high country tended to be windy, but not today. Warm sun, only a touch of wind to blow away the sweat. It wasn't the kind of day when men ought to die.

Slocum went to the front door and rapped twice. It took Darleen Haining a few seconds to open it.

Her eyes went wide as she tried to speak, but no words came out.

"Herk is dead. So is Miles. Him, I shot myself. A bullet in the face ended his trail." Slocum spoke harshly to get the maximum effect.

"Y-you killed them?"

"Aren't you going to invite me inside?" Slocum pushed past her and stood in the cool, dim entryway. He looked around. Sunlight slanted warmly through the window and splashed across the rug on the parlor floor. A hint of furniture polish hung in the air, making this a homey, comfortable, peaceful scene. Slocum knew that appearances were all too often wrong.

He heard the door close and looked over his shoulder. The woman hesitated, her hand on the knob. Then she opened a drawer in a table beside the door. Slocum spun around, ready to throw down on her. His hand curled around the butt of his Colt Navy, then he relaxed.

"A key," she said, holding it up. "I want to ensure our privacy." She locked the door, then put the key back in the drawer. "Why don't you sit down, Mr. Slocum?"

He sat with his back to the window to keep the light from his eyes. He watched as she flittered around, moving this way and that, putting away cleaning rags and the bottle of polish he noticed when he first entered. She was obviously flustered at his unexpected appearance at her front door and wanted a few seconds to compose herself.

"I know about everything," Slocum said. "You were the one who came up with the scheme to high-grade your own husband's mine. Reckon you thought up the idea to have him pay for smelting the ore stolen from under his nose, too."

"You've been a busy boy," she said, standing in the doorway between entry and parlor. "Is Lucas really dead?"

"Dead as a doornail. So's Herk, and Singer is living up to his name. I hope he keeps singing when the marshal finally claps the irons on him."

"He was such a fool," she said. Slocum didn't know which of the men she referred to. And it didn't matter. "But you are obviously very clever. If you had come along sooner, I might have recruited you."

"Where's the gold you got out of the mine? Somewhere on the other side of the mountain is my guess. But did Singer know where you hid it?"

"No, of course not. Neither did Miles. Only Herk and I—" She cut off her confession. "If they're dead, or on their way to jail, that would mean a fifty-fifty split would be quite a haul. I can't get the gold out of the hiding spot by myself, although it always seemed that I did more than Herk ever did when it came to carrying and hiding."

"You offering me half? How much are you talking about?"

"More than a hundred thousand dollars."

"Half of that . . ." Slocum mused.

"No, John—it is John, isn't it? That'd be your half."

Slocum was startled at the sum.

"That's mighty tempting."

"Especially for a man who came begging for a job without even a horse. And there can be other rewards if you help me."

"You offering yourself?"

"I'm *much* better than Evangeline. Don't you think I know how you and that silly girl have been—"

"Never mind her," Slocum said sharply. "I need you to answer one question."

"For you, John, anything." Darleen moved about, her skirts rustling softly. She thrust her leg forward and hiked her skirt to give a hint of ankle. She saw his interest and said, "There's ever so much more. And it'd all be yours."

"And the gold," he said.

Darleen laughed. "Of course, the gold *and* my most intimate favors."

"The question," Slocum said, getting his mind back on the topic. "Why?"

"Why? Why what?"

"Why'd you go to all the trouble of recruiting men like Singer and Miles and seducing Herk? All you'd have to do is ask your husband for money. He'd've given it to you."

"Morgan? Morgan Haining *give* his own wife anything?" She snorted loudly and began pacing to and fro, skirts swishing as she moved. Slocum saw that her expression had changed from fake intimacy to seething hatred. For the first time Slocum felt he was seeing the real woman.

"He's a rich man. He doesn't seem like a penny-pincher."

"Oh, no, Morgan's no miser. That's the problem. He's too generous with the gold. He gives it all away. Do I have a maid to clean and cook? No. He gives every last ounce to men who don't deserve it!"

"Like you do?"

"Yes, dammit, like me!" Darleen Haining raged. "At least I got some small pleasure out of stringing along Singer and Herk and even Miles." Her anger reached epic proportions. "If a man so much as stubs his toe in the mine, Morgan puts him on a lifetime pension. He's got a dozen or more malingerers in that hotel he bought, the place he lets them have room and board for free. And if that's not enough, he pays for their medicine, he pays for their booze, for all I know he pays for their whores!"

"That's why the Low Down is always scraping by," Slocum said, more to himself than Darleen.

"That's right, that's damned right! He thinks nothing of giving away his wealth to men who don't deserve it, but he won't keep a single ounce to support his family. He's never here. He's always thinking up new ways of giving away *my* share of the gold!"

"This is a nice house and you're not starving," Slocum said.

"I want a mansion in Denver. I want servants. Look around. Who does the cleaning? I do. That miserable daughter of his won't lift a finger. No, she's too good. She helps him give away his gold. Gold that by right is *mine!*"

"So you, Herk, and Singer stole it."

"How can you steal what's rightfully yours? It's mine and Morgan was keeping it from me. Why do you think I married him? He owned a mine. How was I to know he gave all the gold from that mine to spendthrifts and wastrels?"

She swung about. Her face was livid but her eyes were cold.

"Kill him, John. Kill him for me so I can inherit it all. Then it'll be just you and me. We can split what I've already taken and the rest will be ours all legal. You'll be a millionaire. And you'll have me!"

"Legal?" said Slocum, shaking his head. "It'd be theft. I'd kill him—then you'd turn me in so you could have it all."

"I knew you were smart. I didn't think you were so smart," she said. Another rustle of her skirt and she lifted a derringer she had hidden in the folds.

"The table beside the door," Slocum said. "Where the key is. You replaced the key and took out the gun."

"So smart and yet so stupid. You think with your balls, just like Miles and Herk and all the rest. No wonder Evangeline couldn't wait to rut with you, you animal!"

"All the rest," Slocum said. His six-shooter could be drawn while he was seated. A cross-draw holster afforded easy accessibility in the saddle or while he was standing on the ground, but he made no move. Darleen had the derringer pointed straight at him, and the look of determination showed she was going to fire.

"Good-bye, Slocum," she said.

"You've got that wrong, Darleen. It's you who's going." Morgan Haining stepped up behind his wife and grabbed her wrist. The derringer discharged into the ceiling.

"You! You!" Darleen looked wildly from her husband to Slocum and back. Then she realized Evangeline was also present and had entered through the back door with her father, listening to every word she had said.

"I hate you all!" Darleen shoved Haining away hard enough to stagger him. Slocum jumped to his feet and whipped out his six-gun, but the report that echoed in the house wasn't from his Colt Navy. The second barrel of the derringer had discharged.

Morgan Haining had grabbed for her again, and the gun had been pressed against her breast when the second chamber discharged. Whether Darleen had fired or Haining had somehow grabbed the weapon, Slocum couldn't tell. From the way Darleen Haining lay slumped on the floor, a bright red spot expanding to stain her blouse just over her heart, he knew it didn't matter.

"Bitch," Evangeline said. She stepped forward as if she intended to kick her dead stepmother, but she stopped a few feet away and stared. Then she threw her arms around her father and held him again, as she had back at the mill.

All Slocum heard was the pair of them softly crying. He slid his six-shooter back into its holster and slipped past them. The key was where Darleen had left it in the drawer beside the door. Slocum unlocked the front door and stepped out into the bright, cheerful Colorado afternoon.

He could take Lucas Miles's horse and no one would care. But he needed a horse he could ride. One of the horses from the ore cart—the one he had saddle-broken—

would do. This horse would be missed, but he doubted Haining would set the sheriff on his trail.

From inside the house he heard father and daughter talking in guarded tones. He didn't want to know what they said to one another.

It was time for him to leave Cripple Creek. Slocum hurried to the stables and put six miles behind him before sundown, glad to leave behind Evangeline, the Low Down Mine, and even the mountain of gold Darleen Haining had stolen.

Watch for

SLOCUM AND THE GILA RIVER HERMIT

342nd novel in the exciting SLOCUM series
from Jove

Coming in August!

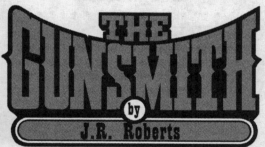

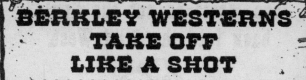